"PEOPLE OF ARCTURUS!

"The time has come. For the past month I have been far away in space, holding conference with the representative of an alien civilization, and I have now returned . . .

"You, as Arcturians, are now in the fore-front of the ranks of humanity. Out of all the civilized planets, it is we who have found the first intelligent alien culture . . .

"Tomorrow . . .
"Tomorrow a representative of this alien race will be here . . .

"Tomorrow the Alien and I will each make a statement on the future of Mankind.

"Tomorrow is the dawn of a new era!"

Tomorrow could also mean the end of man's domination of the stars——but how could Arcturus realize that?

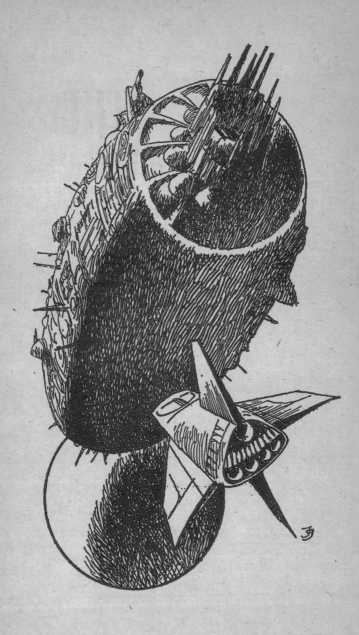

THE
HAWKS
OF
ARCTURUS

by

Cecil Snyder III

DAW BOOKS, INC.
DONALD A. WOLLHEIM, PUBLISHER

1301 Avenue of the Americas
New York, N. Y.   10019

To Candy

FIRST PRINTING, MAY 1974

1 2 3 4 5 6 7 8 9

PRINTED IN U.S.A.

Chapter One

◆

A thin tendril of white smoke, almost invisible in the dim moonlight, broke from the pile of wood shavings and drifted lazily up toward a small patch of open sky.

Leaning closer, his cheek to the ground, he blew gently again. His eyes caught the reflection of a small ember. The smoke made him blink. A tiny dart of flame licked up at him. He leaned back on his haunches with a grunt of satisfaction, pulling a worn brown blanket tight around his back to clutch at his throat. With one hand he ranged dry broken wood in a precise pyramid around the little flame. The fire crackled, not yet radiating much warmth, but bright and smokeless. The circle of tall spruce which ringed the clearing shut out the darkness as it screened the light from the surrounding forest.

When the wood had collapsed onto a bed of red embers, the old man took his pail to the creek which ran along one side of the clearing. The creek lay in darkness between steep banks, waist-high. On the thin margin between the water and the bank, he knelt in the sand to scrub out the pail, rinsed and filled it where the stream ran rapidly amidst the rocks.

Holding the heavy pail out away from his body for balance, the old man scrambled back up the clayey bank. He set the water down by the fire, and walked off into the darkness on the other side of the glade, returning a moment later swinging a hatchet in one hand, and in the other, a long green branch as thick as his arm. He stripped the branch clean, sharpened the thick end, and cut a deep notch near the opposite end. The

5

branch was then secured between two rocks so it angled out over the fire. He hung the pail where it swung impaled by the flames and settled back to wait for it to boil.

The intense heat washed over the coals like water. The old man took off his blanket, folded it, and sat upon it. He was naked except for a broad cloth belt that supported a hatchet and a large canvas pouch. The pail hissed as it heated, and then stopped. The water began to steam. Sweat glinting in the wrinkles on his forehead, the old man seemed to have lost consciousness of his surroundings. The air whisked through the tips of the high pines, undermining the deep silence. There was no hint of sleep in his bright eyes. Hunched up by the fire, hugging his knees to his chest, he was patiently waiting.

The water began to sputter and hiss, coming slowly to a boil. Beyond the receding light of the fire, across the glade where he had learned to expect them, he saw the amber gleam of two immense unwinking eyes.

There was no sound, no hint of movement from within the velvet shadows of the skirt of the giant pine. The old man, avoiding any abrupt movement, began to prepare his supper. He took a paper packet from the canvas pouch at his side and sprinkled its contents, a pungent, crumbling power, onto the roiling surface of the water. He added three whole tubers he had foraged during the day and a large gem of rock salt. Slowly stirring, he looked again into the eyes. They stared back.

The old man settled comfortably back on his heels, and swaying gently back and forth, hummed softly, so softly at first that the sound seemed to come from the treetops. Louder it grew, a deep sawing tone that originated in his belly, reverberating deep in his chest, which his open mouth betrayed only by a slight quivering of the lower lip. The air was cold on his back. The eyes approached.

There was a whisper of movement from the darkness; the amber eyes blinked and were gone. The old man started up, an exclamation of surprise on his lips and disappointment in his eyes.

A cry and a thunderous splash from the stream behind him sent the old man swirling around, as agile as a cat, snatching the hatchet from his belt. In the half-light of the clearing, equal parts of moonlight and firelight, he saw a tall figure, wet to the bones and smeared with clay, stumble up the short bank of the stream.

The intruder was a man of about thirty, with dark chiseled features and coal-black hair that fell to his shoulders in a thousand dripping ringlets. Above his shadowy eyes, which darted quickly around the clearing, was an emerald medallion on a thin chain, the silhouette of a Rimhawk in flight.

The man stood with one foot planted forward, posed to advance or flee. The water ran profusely from his disheveled hair and several layers of brightly patterned clothing.

"Come here. Sit down by the fire," the old man invited. The intruder approached. One hand was concealed under his robe; the other was extended palm-up in the traditional gesture of peace.

"I am looking for the Arcturian Ambassador. At the embassy they told me that he was on leave and I would find him, ah, hereabouts. Do you . . . ?"

"Yes, in fact. I am the Ambassador. Do sit down."

It took all of the visitor's practiced aplomb, already badly shaken by the fall in the stream, not to gape. Then it was true what they had told him about old Reglane, Lord of Intrus and ten years Ambassador to Earth. He was practically naked but for the tattered brown blanket. His ribs stuck out. A sparse beard barely covered his jowls, and his thin hair was tied back so that his brow loomed high above his jutting eyebrows. There was no mistaking that predatory nose.

"Sit down," the old man repeated patiently, but in such a tone that he was instantly obeyed. "You do not know me, perhaps. But I know you, En'varid. I have heard of your rise to prominence in Darlan's burgeoning ranks of opportunists. And I know you come from him. I have been anticipating your message, so I will tell you at once that I serve Arcturus, and not Darlan."

The abruptness and thoroughly undiplomatic frankness of this statement caught En'varid completely off-guard. He searched for a reply. He saw that the old man was slight, but not frail. The skin fit tight on his worn, rounded bones. His mouth, his eyes, were hard and determined.

The Ambassador rose and stirred the contents of his pail with a stick. He took a shallow wooden bowl from his pouch and dipped it into the gruel.

"Supper," he said. "Go on, drink it."

The envoy looked suspiciously at the proffered bowl.

"Go on."

En'varid burned his tongue, but the warmth revived him somewhat. "I have come with a message from Darlan, yes. And a request. A break with the Dominions is eminent. . . ."

The old man did not show his surprise.

"Darlan is about to lead Arcturus off on a path of her own."

"Off the deep end, you mean," the Ambassador interjected.

"He needs the support of every Arcturian. Particularly yours, Ambassador."

"If our new Herald has no confidence in my loyalty, it is his prerogative to replace me. I should be happy to step aside."

"You have been on Earth for ten years. No Arcturian knows as well as you how to find his way through the bureaucratic maze of the Dominion's councils. No one knows as well how to persuade these Earthmen to peacefully leave hold of our planet." En'varid lowered his voice and leaned closer. "You could prevent a struggle which would break the Dominions right down the middle and give way to a devastating internecine war. Darlan's interests are the interests of Arcturus. You would be wise to serve him."

The old man busied himself for a while building up the fire, which had dimmed considerably. He thought, not of his home planet, but of the yellow eyes of the great cat which had disappeared into the forest when En'varid had so rudely interrupted. It was an old, old cat of extraordinary beauty and intelligence. It was on this spot he had met it, years ago, for this was its territory, and he stayed here only by its leave. A close bond had grown between them, a spry old man and a proud old cat. It was no pet. The animal had taught him much, about Earth and about himself.

"The Earth was torn apart once before by the rivalry of men," the Ambassador said softly. "You know that story well. And the first-wave colonials returned to find her like a sponge squeezed of almost all life. For two centuries they worked to rebuild her. They stripped planets of their richest topsoil to restore their home. They brought back to Earth the catalog of plants and animals they had taken with them to nurture under alien suns. Earth soaked it all up; she blossomed as never before."

The old man leaned forward and grasped En'varid by the wrist. "But there is a force here now, a new spirit that has grown up among these plants and men and animals that came back to repopulate a memory. A small link as of yet, spread as thin as a spiderweb. You could not know it, En'varid, for you have not lived here. But you would miss it if Arcturus was to secede from the Dominions of Earth. It is not the enthusiasm of the second-wave colonials who are like bees busy terraforming, nor the staid industrious greed and complacency of the proud first-wave colonials. The Earth has germinated something new from old seeds. Here, time has ... forgiven, you might say, everything." He waved his hand vaguely at the sky. "Out there time merely forgets."

En'varid smiled disdainfully, forgetting for the moment his dripping clothes smeared with clay and the painful bruise on his right knee. "Look at you, Ambassador. Is this what ten years on Earth has done to the most able diplomat Arcturus has ever produced, a scion of one of the founding families, forty years a councilman, ten years a Herald yourself? Squatting in the dirt beside a pile of burning sticks, with a little ax to protect you from the beasts of this forest. ... Is this what Earth offers you, and us?"

"The Earth lives only on the reverence of men, like a parasite on the commerce of the colonies," he said with the assurance of a man delivering a maxim which his experience has confirmed. "She is an old tree fertilized by her own fruit. When new trees push up, she strangles them with her strong old roots. We *must* push her aside, can't you see? And we will, too, for we have the power, and power knows no precedence. We will smash her like a hollow gourd if she dares deny us!"

"Calm down, En'varid," the Ambassador cautioned. He paused. "I am an old man, ninety years old. When I was young, Huget swarmed through our sector with ships and soldiers like locusts. Arcturus was slowly developing, a land of orchards and wheatfields. If we weak agricultural planets had not united then under the banner of Earth, we would not now be in a position to use our liberty to defy her.

"And now Arcturus would impose her rule as Huget once tried—do not deny it—gathering our weaker neighbors under our wing. Would this economic and military imperialism not be harsher than the cultural imperialism of Earth? And do you think the other first-wave planets which rank not far behind our own wealth and power will take this lying down? Either they will unite to help Earth squash Arcturus, turn her back into a farm, or they will follow your lead and turn the civilized galaxy into a score of dissenting empires. Do you wish to rip the flower of mankind apart by the petals, En'varid?"

"No!" En'varid sprang to his feet. "Arcturus *will* unite the galaxy under the banner of the Rimhawk. We do not mistake age for wisdom. We will take the initiative. We have the power!"

He seemed so sure. Could Darlan really pull it off? the Ambassador wondered. His abrupt rise to power in the chaotic politics of Arcturus had been nothing less than astounding. But Arcturus was just one colony out of more than five hundred. The hand of man reached with many fingers toward the heart of the galaxy, yet they were still just on the shores of a teeming mass of stars. Nowhere had any creature stood up to the vainglory of man—who wandered alone among the stars—and said, "Here you must stop!" Even if he did have the power, could Darlan replace the authority of Earth like a new glove on the hand of man; or was Earth the very flesh of the hand?

Living on the mother planet, the Ambassador had begun to understand the purpose which gave the internal cohesion to the image of Earth, the idea of Man. Stirring far down in the Earth, he could feel the thought that moved them all, solid rock, wood, and flesh. The old cat was beginning to lead him to it. But how could he explain it to this crass first-wave colonialist, this magnetism that held them all together? Indeed, maybe it was just old age twisting and teasing his mind, a teleological fancy. These native Earthmen, did they see it? It was so hard to get through to them. The Ambassador almost sighed.

"You may tell Darlan that he will find me a difficult tool to use, for I am sure he will have trouble finding my handle."

"Our Herald anticipated that I might have to use more than words to persuade you." The old man looked sharply at him. "I am going to divulge a great secret to you, Ambassador. You must pledge me your discretion. Your treason would aid Earth little anyway."

"Of course, you have my word."

"You are certain there is no one about?" En'varid wished he was in a room, any room, not exposed thus to the black forest and open sky.

"There are few forest people around here, and they aren't interested in secrets. Indeed, you would be hard put to find one, for they avoid strangers like the plague."

From an inner pocket of his cape En'varid produced a small pouch of chain mesh. He opened the voice-lock with three sibilant phonemes that the Ambassador could not have reproduced and took out a flat metal box, about three inches square and a half-inch thick. The box had a dull silver sheen and was featureless except for two ball bearings the size of peas set in sockets in opposite corners.

The Ambassador peered intently at it in the flickering light of the fire. Was it a weapon? "May I?" he asked, and reached over and gingerly took the box. It was as light as though it had been made of puffed cotton. It practically floated right out of his hand. The box felt alive—not quite quivering, not quite vibrating, but somewhere between the animal and the mechanical.

"Hold it so." En'varid held up his hand to demonstrate. "With your thumb and finger on the balls."

The Ambassador put it in position. It looked as though it would slip out of his hand, but it didn't.

"What does it do?"

"It remembers," En'varid said.

The box began to spin on the bearings, gradually picking up speed. The whirling metal blurred, and an intense light broke through in places, like the sun breaking through the clouds. The light caught the old man's eyes; he was drawn out. En'varid, leaning forward; the circle of pines; the pale sky and bright fire—all grew dim. But he remembered all so clearly. . . .

He was walking fast among the towering ferns, trying to outpace his anger. In the back of his mind, Ra still mocked his fierce postures. "You are a warrior, Luxor. You will never change. But there is no need, now, for warriors." She mouthed the epithet as if it were quaint, almost archaic. "We have uprooted the tree of war. It will bear fruit no more."

From the very first, before they had even made their disastrous planetfall, they had been constantly drumming on the subject of his uselessness. For he was the last. Ten stern warriors there had been. Four had gone in the shattering tidal wave of gas from their own blasted sun. They were three light-years away, but it hit them hard.

You can see novas all the time. They are the most magnificent fireworks of space. But this was their sun, the hub of the Five Systems. Now Selenor itself had been swallowed whole by the swollen sun, and the twelve planets of their five closely interlocked star systems were sent reeling head-over-heels out into space.

Outward bound in search of a new world when the disaster struck, they had been caught like a leaf in a hurricane and swept far beyond their goal in a crippled ship, their cancerous sun falling fast to the rear.

And they had found ... paradise! Any barren piece of land would have seemed a godsend to the broken ranks of unhappy refugees, but this was a fertile, temperate world of broad forests and wide rivers, young and peaceful and swarming with life, with rich air and an abundance of edible plants. He looked around the forest of ferns. The warm late-afternoon sun was slanting through a yellow-green canopy of lacy leaves and dangling bursts of white blossoms. The floor was spread with broad reddish leaves, perfectly round and over an arm's length in diameter, the foilage of the yo flower, a blue crescent on a tall, willowy stalk. The land was ripe for farmers and builders.

And there was nothing bigger than a jellyfish to harm them.

The colonists had lost but a few on landing, but in this group were five more of the warrior caste. And when the ship was safely down, like a whale beached and broken on the shore, the preordained hierarchy of the colonists took over. It was a utilitarian order—the more useful you were, the more weight your opinion carried. And he was the only one who was demonstrably useless. They had taken his weapons and smelted them down to make something serviceable. He fashioned himself a spear, ridiculous but somehow reassuring as he prowled the outskirts of the settlement. Going on patrol, he would say. Taking a walk, they would say.

Finally Ra, new mother of twin girls, had persuaded the council to take away his spear. "I'll have no weap-

ons around my children," she argued. There was no
gainsaying her. She was obviously quite functional.

The sun was growing bigger now as it dropped down
into the forest, lighting the underside of the leaves. As
his anger cooled, he was thinking of the old enemy, his
enemy. They were all dead, he supposed, their neighboring star system ripped apart in the cataclysm. They
lived on only in his memory. Now he was indeed the
last warrior, the end of a world.

As he turned from anger to sorrow, he slackened his
pace till he was strolling slowly amidst the ferns. He
came to a familiar glade, where, after a short pause and
a drink from a small stream, he would customarily turn
back, arriving at the settlement just after dark. This
time he kept on past the brief sandy clearing. He
couldn't face another dinner in the crowded hall, listening to the uniformly enthusiastic reports of the useful
members of the settlement. He would sleep against the
fluted bole of a fern that night. There was nothing to be
afraid of, not in this damned park!

By dark, he was well into a part of the forest he had
never before penetrated. The sun thickened and disappeared quickly, but before it had completely set, the
stars came out like a handful of bright silver dust
strewn across the sky. It was called the Veil of Tears,
the near center of the galaxy, a nub of stars so bright
that they did not allow any more than a pale twilight to
fall over the forest. He paused at the crest of a jagged
ridge which allowed him an unimpeded view of the
heavens. His people had always worshiped the stars,
but no more.

Soon it rose, a smear of brilliant light. Already the
cloud was burning less bright, and in its heart a faint
dot could be made out, like the nucleus of a crabbed
nerve cell, their spent sun, the bloodless fire that had
consumed five neighboring star systems, an ancient civilization, his home, his family.

The others were lucky, no doubt. They had come as
families, looking forward. He had expected to return to
his family, with news of the colony and a cargo of nov-

elties. He took it personally. It was like the universe had slapped him in the face.

Stretched out on the mossy turf, he dozed off for a short while. When he awoke, he was thirsty, and his solitary brooding suddenly seemed ridiculous. He decided to find a small stream to quench his thirst and then set off for the settlement. He followed the slope of the ridge down to his left, emerging abruptly from the heavy growth by a small pond with a clear border of low grass. Without hesitation, he knelt on the bank. The pond was clear and deep, with a rough, rocky floor ten feet down. He took off his light, close-fitting helmet of burnished golden metal as supple as leather, the one badge of rank left him. In a characteristic gesture, he rubbed his head, and dipped the helmet into the water, swishing it around to rinse it out.

He froze suddenly, as an animal or a trained soldier. Had he heard a noise? He shrugged. He always got jumpy in the aftermath of these arguments with Ra.

As he bent to refill his helmet, a heavy blow struck him between the shoulderblades, sprawling him half into the pool. His cry drowned in the cold. His helmet settled gently down into the crystal water; he plunged down into a great gap. . . .

The Ambassador found himself facing En'varid in the flickering shadows of the forest clearing. The gap crashed down on him, like a wave he had ridden to shore. He nearly blacked out from the dizzying reorientation. With a visible effort he calmed the surging nausea. He lay back on the rough grass and looked at the small patch of stars hemmed in by the pines, at riderless Pegasus winging his still way across the night sky. En'varid, who had pulled the box from his hand when he saw terror shake the slumbering face of the old man, locked it back in its pouch and secreted it in an inner pocket of his rumpled cape.

The old man was thinking about the stars. The rest of the—vision?—did not make sense to him yet, but he was quick to grasp the significance of the dazzling night sky. He had been taken to the heart of the galaxy, many light-years beyond the farthest frontiers of the Dominions.

In his memory he looked through alien eyes again. From the time of the Great Breakout man had longed for—and dreaded—his first contact with other intelligent life. And now Darlan had somehow stumbled on man's passkey to the galaxy, and the Ambassador doubted if there was a less deserving man in all the Dominions. Perhaps fledgling humanity was on trial for its life even now before the tribunals of an older and stronger civilization, with Darlan as its advocate. And what response could man expect when the only question Darlan ever asked was, "Are you stronger than I?"

The Ambassador got unsteadily to his feet and pulled his blanket tight around his back. The fire was dying. He fed it and blew upon the coals until the fresh wood had burst into flame. En'varid regarded him closely, anxious to know what impression the "memories"—if such vivid re-creation could be described so lightly—had made on the old diplomat. The Ambassador was tempted to ask his visitor, beg him, to tell all he knew of this alien culture, but he hesitated. The knowledge would have its price, he knew. Darlan's price.

En'varid was feeling the chill now, for his silks were still damp from his fall in the stream. The medallion on his forehead flashed with a hard metallic luminosity that was out of place among the pines.

"Ambassador?" he asked softly.

"You will convey my respects to Darlan, our new Herald," the Ambassador said shortly, "and tell him I await his instructions. I expect to have the fullest details on this civilization with which Darlan has made contact."

"You shall, Ambassador. You will hear from us shortly." With a stiff bow, En'varid took his leave, returning the way he had come, fording the stream, to disappear into the pines.

The old man took the gruel remaining in his pail and poured it onto the smoldering fire. He wasn't hungry. A great cloud of steam rose in the air. He idly stirred the water into the ashes. A tremendous headache hammered at the base of his skull.

At length, when he looked up again, the giant eyes of the great cat were looking at him from across the stream. Their narrow gaze was questioning and accusatory.

En'varid was relieved to secure himself in the warm, orderly confines of his flitter. He had lost his way twice in the dark, and thought someone or something had been tailing him, though frequent glances had discovered nothing lurking behind him. He settled himself into the control seat and turned up the thermostat, for he was shivering.

When he had set a course for Old Port, he took the chain-mesh pouch from his cape and sat weighing it in his hand without opening it. Darlan was little fit to use this, he reflected. No, he was a monomaniac adept only in the application of political power, an infighter. When En'varid had consolidated the power of the Herald, Darlan's usefulness would be at an end. En'varid would find a way to dispose of him; he already had several tentative schemes in mind. When it came to the crux, the powerful families of Arcturus would surely unite behind one of their own, not a political black sheep. En'varid studied his distorted reflection in the plexiglass bubble of the flitter. En'varid Herald, he mouthed the words softly, testing them. En'varid Herald.

Chapter Two

The *Astrion* was the oldest starliner on the K5 quadrant run, dating back, some said, to the resettlement of Earth. In the course of two centuries she had been rebuilt and refurbished countless times, till little remained of the original ship save its vast untarnished durallum shell. The shell itself, a perfect sphere more than ten miles in circumference, was obscured by a multitude of random additions: observation blisters, Gothic spires of glittering chromium, the lacy bowls of radiometric screens. One triangular portion of the hull was cloaked in a dense forest of oak, elm, and birch, preserved by the windless vacuum of space for eternity. Amidst the trees rose four or five luxurious lodges where from your bedroom window—which, however, did not open—you could watch a never-ending succession of brilliant unwinking stars rise and set over the still leaves and unrumpled lawn.

Chen rolled his tiny ship slowly around the edge of the orbiting starliner till he spotted the large inverted cone that was the landing dock. He connected with the *Astrion*'s controller and punched his astrogator for receive. The *Astrion*'s copilot took control of his surveyor, and Chen settled back in his chair, enjoying the view now that he could devote his whole attention to it. His ship settled slowly tail-first down into the cone. There was a muted clang, and the screens went dark. The ship was enclosed in the webbing of a cylindrical metal capsule. The capsule shot down a tube. When it opened, two huge black waldos on rubbery arms picked up his ship as gently as a fat woman lifts a cream puff.

The tender floated up level with a rack the size of a football field and deposited Chen's ship alongside more than a score of vessels of a similar size.

When he felt the ship settle to rest, Chen began the detailed and tedious procedure for shutting the surveyor down for the duration of the voyage of the *Astrion*, damping her power, shorting her circuits, and plunging the various brains that ran the ship into a deep and dreamless sleep. The reassuring syncopation of ticks and hums faded into silence; the long rows of lights on the control board blinked out as he shut down the systems, circuit by circuit. In the dim blue glow of the single standby light he could not resist murmuring "Good-bye" before he leaped out onto the resilient surface of the landing shelf.

From outside he looked over the surveyor admiringly. She was sixty feet of shimmering durallum, seamless and featureless except for the fiercely glowering eyes painted on either side of her needle-nose, and between these, across the bridge of her nose, the identification letters DS-48. He had painted the eyes himself just three days ago, after the last trial run had been made and the sale consummated. He still had not recovered from the first flushed pride of ownership. This was the newest, fastest, sturdiest surveyor you could buy, and he had sunk the entire proceeds of his last claim—a trillion-ton asteroid of ninety-eight-per-cent-pure crystalline selenium in the Centuri quadrant—in her purchase and outfitting. He had fuel and supplies for one standard Earth year out of Arcturus, and if he had hit nothing by then . . .

A small shuttlecar came down behind him with a faint hiss of airjets, hovering a foot off the surface. Chen vaulted into the open car, and it took off again with a sigh, angling down past several shelves on which a wide variety of ships were ranged: excursion "skippers," shuttles, surveyors, deep-space yachts, auxiliary waldos, and others whose use even Chen's experienced eyes could not guess.

There were four other passengers on the circular

bench of the shuttlecar. To Chen's right were two Mandarks, husband and wife apparently, their skin-tight garments trimmed with white feathers. Their dark eyes carefully avoided his gaze. But the two other passengers eyed Chen curiously. They were apparently together, Chen surmised, but not intimate (at least, not publicly). They sat not too close, but not too far apart, just so. The woman was remarkably beautiful, tall and long-legged, her willowy figure dressed in an aluminized pilot's liner like the one Chen himself wore. Her prominent cheekbones underlined immense eyes of amber flicked with black. Her eyebrows were very light, almost perfect semicircles. Her hair was cropped shoulder-length, framing her pale forehead in a Gothic arch that accentuated its height. She looked at Chen frankly, with no hint of coyness. He realized he was staring, and turned his eyes on her companion.

This man was even taller, imposing. Though Chen did not remark it, there was even a vague resemblance between himself and this stranger. They both had the same cleft in the chin, the same straight-and-narrow nose, and dark piercing eyes. But Chen's mouth was full and mobile, while the woman's companion had a thin, taut mouth that was fixed and grim. His dark hair was elaborately curled, spread out on the shoulders of a deep crimson cape which swept from his tight high collar uninterrupted to his feet, covering all but the blue toes of his leather boots.

On his forehead he wore the medallion of the Rimhawk. He looked Chen over with the practiced disdain of one who was born rich in the world where money is the measure of a man.

His stern gaze annoyed Chen. Money did not awe him, nor nobility. This man might own a sizable chunk of some planet, but from orbit any planet was just another piece of dirt rolling in the sky, another dot on his charts, not even visible from a light-year away.

Chen stayed in space as much as he could. He had seen many planets, but preferred to spend his idle time floating around them in the great orbital cities that supplied spacers with everything from nucleoids to chewing gum. Once a man had "shaken off the dirt," it was not easy for him to adapt himself to life planetside again. The orbital cities had their own unique society and customs. They were a civilization apart. Between any two free cities there was more of a bond, no matter how vast the distance separating them, than between the city and its parent planet. Notwithstanding the bond of necessity that committed them each to each, spacers did not like "dirtcroppers"—no matter how wealthy—any more than the planet-bound colonials liked these men who roam the cold vacuum beyond their laws and customs.

Chen looked at the frayed elbows of his suit liner, where the printed circuits showed like silver veins through the aluminase. Dirtcroppers said that the vast blackness and solitude drove spacers into amoral atavism. They were human beasts that hid under a veneer of technical sophistication. The time Chen had spent in Old Port had not been enjoyable. It had taken him two months to peddle his claim to a "shaker"—a middleman who would spend more time and effort than Chen could spare finding a developer. Another week was spent acquiring and outfitting his new ship. The old one sat in a shop with a repair bill for more than that time-beaten old hulk was worth. Chen spent days lying on his back in his hotel bed staring out the window at the stained and rain-streaked wall of the next building. He had not changed his tarnished liner the whole time he was there. The back was polished shiny by long hours of sitting in hard wooden chairs, the elbows and knees frayed, revealing the truth of that old homily, "Every liner has a silver lining."

The shuttlecar came to rest lightly on a small platform. Chen waited for the other passengers to debark, following them out with his eyes. The woman smiled broadly as she passed. He winked, and watched her as she followed the tall man in red to a tube marked UP.

Chen's room was an old one, deep in the interior of the *Astrion*. It smelled of stale tobacco smoke and mildew. There were no windows, but the ceiling of the bedroom, when the polarization was switched off, looked up on the elaborate floating garden that filled the weightless core of the ship. The room was spacious, though dirty. The bed was unmade and the sheets yellowed, crumpled in a heap. He checked the bathroom. The tiles of the shower were grimy with the dirt of the fourteen worlds of the Earth-Arcturus run. A broken perfume bottle was swept into a corner, and the air was heavy with musk.

He stretched out on the bed, looking up through the ceiling at the passengers circulating idly through the garden. The foliage and flowers were brightly illuminated by the light of Sol, which fell down a broad shaft that was turned sunward. He was feeling a familiar queasiness, a faint emptiness. The long weeks of waiting were finally drawing to a close. He felt like a high diver bouncing on the end of the board before he takes the long plunge into empty space.

He waited awhile. When the crowd in the garden thinned out a bit, he found his way up to the core of the ship.

In the near-silence he was surprised to hear the calls of birds. As a dog is to a farmer, so is a bird to a lonely spaceman. Chen felt his anxiety draining out of him. Creepers trailed through the air, unattached, in all directions. Using these to guide himself, he floated in toward the center of the garden.

He knew what he would find there. It was in the exact center of the garden, and therefore in the exact center of the ship. The creepers, flowers and bushes stopped short; it was framed in empty space, slowly revolving, a huge flower of crystal.

It had been found drifting aimlessly in the ungodly vacuum of interstellar space, out far beyond Arcturus. It was shaped like a shallow bowl, about twelve feet across. From the inside of this bowl grew an exquisite profusion of crystal spikes of varied lengths, from a full foot long to the size of a rose thorn. The bottom of the bowl was perfectly smooth, and faintly warm to the touch. The whole mass was a pure crystal, shot through with all the vivid brilliance of which the spectrum is capable. And the colors, as you looked, could be seen to shift, so slowly, like the turning of the minute hand of a clock.

It was pure crystallized helium, it had been ascertained, from some unknown solar system, or perhaps from the heart of a dead star, extracted by some magic, like ambergris from the corpse of a whale. Scientists had come from a score of planets to examine it. It was the subject of a dozen scholarly articles. But in the end it proved a better tourist attraction than a scientific mantelpiece. Some people, the crewmen of the *Astrion* would assure you, had taken passage just to get a look at it. Scientific speculation had come to an abrupt end when the captain of the *Astrion* had found some scientists trying their best to break off a piece of it—unsuccessfully—and had them rather ignominiously thrown off the ship.

As Chen contemplated the massive glowing gem with his chin sunk on his chest, he was startled by a soft "Hello." He turned and looked directly into two large amber eyes flecked with black. She smiled. He looked around for her companion in the red cape, but the garden was apparently empty except for the two of them.

"I thought everyone had gone topside to watch the lift-off."

Chen smiled awkwardly, feeling vaguely apprehensive. "I was admiring the flowers. Largest free-floating garden in interstellar space, the brochure says."

"This flower?" she asked.

"The stoneflower, yes. Do you know of it?"

She didn't answer. She was studying the brilliant coruscations of lambent flame which played on the surface of the crystal. She seemed to draw herself away from some memory. "Are you a pilot?"

"I'm a prospector, name of Chen." This distinction was important: a pilot flew someone else's ship; a prospector flew his own. "You may have seen my ship from the shuttlecar. New Durry-Sundial surveyor. The one with the eyes."

"My name is Alsar. I am the personal pilot of Lord En'varid, secretary to the Herald of Arcturus."

Chen showed his surprise. "Then he's as important as he looks."

"Even more," Alsar assured him. "You don't know Arcturus very well, do you?"

"No. My first run into that quadrant. I was prospecting out of Centauri before. Sites make a better percentage out there, closer to the tradeways. But that area is getting well picked over. Cartels are mopping up with auto-surveyors now. . . ."

"Why did you choose Arcturus?" she asked. "You could have picked a quieter sector, my friend. That planet isn't getting on all that well with the rest of the Dominions right now."

"Oh?" Chen remarked absently. "I don't know much about politics. Scarcely look at a video. Doesn't concern me. Just going on a hunch, actually." He wasn't accustomed to talking over his motives or intentions. No sensible prospector ever divulged his sources or his itinerary, even to a friend, and anyone pumping Chen for information was likely to meet with dead silence, if not open hostility. He looked away to the flower with narrowed eyes.

"Tell me about the flower," Alsar suggested.

"It was found by a prospector more than thirty years ago, drifting in deep space. He sold it to the *Astrion* as a display piece. It used to draw quite a crowd. It's alive, in a fashion. They tried to take it apart once. Couldn't break it, though. The novelty wore off. People have mostly forgotten about it by now."

"You seem to know a lot about it," Alsar said. "It must have been found before you were born."

He hesitated. "I knew the man who discovered it."

"You did? Is he still alive?"

Chen didn't answer. A recurrent waking dream flashed through his mind. He stood in a white room.

The hairless old man, propped up in bed, was pushing
the air back with shaking hands, seeking to defend
himself from some remembered demon, reliving the
disaster which had broken him. He tried to speak, his
eyes rolled up till only the whites showed, as pale as his
face. His back arched up off the bed. An attendant
dressed in white came in and strapped the invalid down
efficiently and then left without a word, as if he had
important business elsewhere which he had momentarily interrupted. After a while the old man quieted and
sank into a deep sleep. Chen stood rooted to the spot.
They said it did the old prospector good to relive his
nightmares, reestablished his emotional equilibrium.
They didn't know how bad it was. In his saner moments the old man couldn't bear to talk about it, not
even to his adopted son. But each time Chen came to
see him, he begged for the sedation the hospital
wouldn't give him, begged with tears running down his
face, broken of the last vestiges of pride and dignity.
His reputation had once spanned half the civilized
galaxy. Chen slipped him sleeping pills now and then,
to ease his misery. How was he to know the old man
was hoarding them, till one day he had enough? That
was all. They found him curled up like a baby, hugging
his pillow. . . .

"What?"

"I said, would you like to go have a last look at
Sol?" Alsar repeated. "We can make it before the lift-
off if we hurry."

They made their way through the garden to the
shaft. There was a platform upon which they fell
lightly. A long spiral stair wound down the shaft. As
they descended, they could feel the gravity swelling, till
near the floor it was almost a full Earth-gee, due not to
centrifugal force but to the powerful nuclear gravity accelerators which lay under the skin of the *Astrion.* The
intense sunlight filled the shaft with a golden mist,
brimming up from the huge disk of fire which the lens
mellowed and dispersed. Alsar told him about the
hard-edged blue-white sun of Arcturus. It was a planet

of sharp shadows, of small seas and vast plains, once
an agricultural monotony, now laid over with a heavy
grid of industry.

There was a large group of people standing on the
clear floor at the bottom of the shaft. The sun directly
underneath made their silhouettes small and dark, like
flies on a windowpane. When they reached the floor,
Alsar and Chen could see the immense bulk of Earth
posed to their right, half-obscured by the near horizon
of the ship itself. A great storm was spread out over all
of the visible northern hemisphere, covering the land-
mass entirely, trailing its long arms over the pole and
down toward the equator. Alsar's downy hair seemed
to trap the sunlight and send it spinning in all directions.

Chen felt a familiar tinge of nausea. "We're about to
move."

A dumpy matron anxiously caught hold of her companion's arm. "Oh, dear! We're falling!" The Earth
seemed to shrink down into a hole in the vast expanse
of velvet space. The sun set over the horizon of the
ship as they turned away from it, and the moon rose,
stark and gaunt, its shadows unshielded by atmosphere
or aurora. On the shores of the Sea of Tranquillity, a
three-square-mile patch of tessellated metal caught the
sun, flashing like cut crystal in a setting of rough rock:
Armansport, named for the leader of the Resettlement.
The newer moon cities, mostly devoted to mining, bur-
rowed into the solid rock, or sealed off one of the vast
natural caves. They gave little hint of their existence on
the surface. But Armansport basked in the light of the
sun, which the returned colonists had traveled so far to
see again. And the ruined, poisoned Earth had ridden
at high noon in the black sky and in their dreams every
day till they had made her whole once again.

Alsar held her breath as the moon seemed to come
straight for them, veering off at the last minute in a
white blur. She caught hold of Chen's arm as though to
steady herself.

Like a ship feeling her way out of a busy harbor, the *Astrion* slowly passed out of the solar system, the sun dwindling to a small yellow dot. Then the ship rocked momentarily, as if cresting a wave, and became calm again.

Chen didn't notice when they went into overdrive. He was lying on his bed again, staring at the blank ceiling. For the twentieth time, he remembered the white blur of the most beautiful moon in the galaxy, and the faint touch of Alsar's hand.

Chapter Three

Chen dried off hastily with a towel that was small and threadbare. With the water still trickling down his back he unwrapped a small blue-paper package and took out the suit he had rented for the duration of the voyage. There was a voluminous pair of orange pants that hung down to his ankles (was that the fashionable length, or just a bad fit?), and a tight-fitting gray shirt with trailing cuffs. A soft rounded white collar hung down in front like a bib. Finally there was a great cape of sheer sky-blue silk, which the tailor had assured him would glow softly in the dark. Chen combed his damp hair and short beard. He hadn't been so clean since Inman's funeral, he thought.

Turning to leave, he paused with his hand on the doorknob. He went and pulled his short-barreled pistol from the pocket of his liner. It was light in the palm of his hand. Wouldn't be likely to need it, he decided. Besides, the orange pants didn't have pockets, and the sheer cape would not hide it. He thrust the gun under the pillow and left, locking the door behind him.

Half-hoping he would run into Alsar again, Chen
drifted through the great floating garden. The spiraling
promenades were crowded with passengers, their brilliant gossamers competing with the flowers; their muted
words were cut off amidst the foliage. He made a quick
circuit of the garden, but could not find her. He wandered aimlessly along the broad concourses for the next
hour, getting acquainted with the old ship, studying the
crowd, eavesdropping, humming a banal tune he had
picked up somewhere. He drifted through several up-
per-level bars where the franchised barkeeps kept up
bustling trade in tax-free drinks and smokes. There
were not many women. Travelers told impossible stories and ethnic jokes. The off-duty crewmen played
cards with concentration. At each bar Chen filled his
long-stemmed pipe with a mixture of tobacco and
rumpweed and smoked it in a corner. He looked as
though he were waiting for someone, but he was just
killing time, lost in the back pages of his memory while
the present turned unnoticed into the past.

He made his way down through the different levels
into the thin rind of first class, stopping now and then
at the elaborate parties which overflowed from the
wealthy staterooms out into the corridors. There were
more women here, and some were attracted to this
young man who seemed to walk on the lively liquid
ambience without falling in. He would talk for a bit,
then suddenly disappear into the crowd.

Following two underdressed, overscented ladies of a
certain age, Chen came to the entrance of one of the
luxurious lodges that rose amid the frozen forest on the
exterior of the hull. It was a simple pit in the floor,
ringed by a low balustrade of polished brass. A small
plaque read "En'varid of Arcturus" in embossed letters.
The noise of a large party came from below. Chen
vaulted over the rail and dropped into the hole. It was
about twenty feet deep. Halfway down, the gravity
equated, and he came to a bobbing halt. He turned
head-over-heels and grabbed the ladder and climbed
up. He emerged in a spacious oak-paneled hall crossed

by thick beams under a lofty ceiling. A swirling crowd clustered in groups around tables of food and drink scattered throughout the room. There were many rich vacationers, merchants, ship's officers, and a sizable contingent of Arcturians distinguished by their elaborately curled hair. Many people had wandered in, as Chen, attracted by the music and the free food and drinks. Adjoining the large hall was a smaller, plush gaming room. The percentage from the gaming tables paid for the food and entertainment, and usually even reimbursed the voyager for the large initial expense of renting the lodge, which also contained living quarters, a private theater, pool, and library. It left the ship's company free to concentrate on running the vessel without having to worry about entertaining their passengers as well.

The vast hall was softly lit by hooded lamps suspended low over the tables. The loft of the hall was lost in darkness, the rough-hewn beams standing out against the shadows. At one end of the hall a great gilded Rimhawk hung from the wall. At the opposite end a large replica of the planet of Arcturus revolved slowly in midair with no apparent support. On its surface, three oceans and a single small polar icecap glittered between minuscule mountains and canals that crisscrossed the green plains like silver threads.

Looking around, Chen noted with distaste that En'varid employed servants in preference to servos. This was not just a wealthy affectation; it was a direct contravention of the Armansport Convention of 57 A.R., which only someone as powerful as this Arcturian could ignore with impunity.

He felt a tug at his long cuff. "Why, Chen, what are you doing here?" There was a gentle mocking in her voice.

"Hello, Alsar." His eyes ran carelessly down her body. Her front was bare from neck to navel. She wore high-waisted tights of a reptilian hide, blue with bands of orange, and her hair was tucked up in a matching helmet of the same supple hide. A light cloak of orange hung from her shoulders. Her eyes were awake and aware, like a snake's.

"Come on. You almost missed the entertainment." She took his hand and led him through the dense crowd down the hall. "Not many spacemen among this crowd. Tourists, gamblers, merchants, and En'varid's political cronies. How did you happen by?"

"I was looking for you."

She didn't answer. At this end of the hall, under the golden emblem of the Rimhawk, the floor sloped gently down to afford a good view of a round sunken expanse of crumpled yellow sand surrounded by a thick glass wall more than ten feet high. On the smooth lip of the glass a Rimhawk perched unconcernedly, preening its blue-black feathers, stopping now and then to sweep the crowd with its cold, lidless, crimson eyes.

Before the coming of the first starships the Rimhawks had ruled Arcturus from the skies. After many colonists had been shred by that scimitar beak and claws like scythes, and after practically every Rimhawk had been shot from the sky, the two species had come to an accord. They made better pets than dogs, some said. Pets? Chen thought the cold eyes reflected nothing but death.

The crowd stood respectfully back from the hawk's perch. Alsar advanced to the front. As she emerged, the Rimhawk took off, its shadow flitting over them, and circled above the upturned faces of the crowd.

From the sand pit there was a rustle, and the sand shifted, uncovering the thick coils of a long snake. A great square head a foot across rose from among the yellow coils, and before most of the crowd had even noticed the yellow snake emerging from the sand, it struck straight at them. The monstrous head crashed into the glass wall opposite Chen with a muted thud that shook the floor. The guests fell over each other in their haste to back away. Alsar turned her head to look at Chen, who was frozen on the spot.

"Impressive, isn't it?" she asked nonchalantly.

The snake drew back to strike again, but suddenly it

caught sight of the Rimhawk circling above, a shadow flickering between the rafters. The crowd was forgotten. A long line of four-inch spikes sprang erect along the spine of the snake. On its head a circlet of spikes curved out like the points of a jester's cap. The huge snake curled up, its barbs protruding in all directions. Still as a rock, only its great eyes revolved as it followed the Rimhawk's flight across the ceiling. Its red-tipped crown sparkled like crystal in the spotlights. The hawk glided in ever-narrower circles, increasing its speed. Folding its wings back, it plummeted directly for the head of the sandsnake. The wings fanned out at the last moment, beating almost upon the spikes, and the Rimhawk swooped up as if it had bounced off. The snake made a quick, almost involuntary jerk after the bird, but did not strike.

The Rimhawk circled lazily once again, increasing its speed, till it struck suddenly from another angle, backing off at the last moment. This maneuver was repeated four times. At each rush the snake grew more unquiet. It quivered with repressed tension.

On the fifth rush, the snake uncoiled with startling speed. In the blur of motion, it seemed as if the snake had pocketed the bird whole in its unhinged, gaping mouth. Sand flew over the crowd as the snake stood extended more than ten feet in the air.

But the Rimhawk, in a move too fast to follow, had flipped under the outspread jaws, clutching at the soft throat that it had enticed the snake to reveal. Steel claws carved the soft skin as the hawk beat its wings about the head of the snake, deafening, blinding, as it held its victim stretched helpless in the air, where it could get no purchase. The curving beak bent under. The tail of the snake flailed at the sand, splashing bucketfuls over the glass wall into the dazed and gaping audience.

Without warning, the serpentine coils fell wriggling spasmodically onto the sand. The Rimhawk rebounded into the air. It shook its head, and the huge severed blockhead of the snake flew over Chen's head, to land with a loud thud in the back of the crowd. A woman screamed and fainted. Then there was dead silence. Chen felt a touch, and looked down to see a viscous drop of blood run off his sleeve and fall to the floor with an audible plop.

The Rimhawk glided to a perch on one of the dark beams and recommenced its preening. Everyone started talking at once. In the commotion, a good number of the throng left to seek tamer entertainment elsewhere. Others drifted off to the adjoining gaming room. Some stayed in the hall talking excitedly about the sport, glancing now and then at the sand pit, where the headless snake twitched, or at the cleanly severed head, rolled up against the leg of an abandoned table of canapés, and then at the rafters, where the dark silhouette of the Rimhawk watched over them.

Chen and Alsar retreated to the opposite end of the hall, under the revolving sphere of Arcturus.

"I'm sure En'varid got a thrill out of that," Alsar said. "He likes to tell the story of how his hawk—he trained it himself—once dropped a sandsnake's head right into the lap of a visiting dignitary from Earth. The poor man shit in his pants."

"He has a peculiar sense of humor, your employer."

"He is quite nasty—for a diplomat. Not all Arcturians are diplomats, though."

"Do you enjoy working for him?"

"Oh, I was up for bid, you know. He bid the highest. I'd find it hard to get a job outside the guild if I didn't honor his offer."

"I wouldn't think you'd let yourself be forced . . ."

"He does pay quite well," Alsar said. "And he makes a better friend than an enemy, too."

"Is he your friend?"

Alsar just smiled. Careful, Chen reminded himself. Everyone has his secrets.

"He thinks he is." She shrugged. "Would you like to gamble? I happen to know that En'varid's push-pull machines are likely to offer you favorable odds tonight.

People remember the first night. They keep coming back for many more, even when the odds get ruinous."

With her hair tucked under the sleek cap, there was something puzzling, intriguing about her, which her open manner sought to belie. Her eyes, with black flecks swimming in amber, or sometimes the amber swimming in the black, seemed to touch him here and there, probing softly like fingers of water. They were hypnotic, half-veiled, with a broad iris that almost effaced the white. When the black predominated, as it did now, they reminded Chen of the vast eye of empty space, with all the suns shining across a broad valley of absolute nothing.

An hour and more of play on the ornate machines of chance left Chen's head throbbing from the variety of flashing lights, spinning sounds, smells, and even slight electrical shocks which the machines gave off in an effort to excite, entice, and entrap the user. They had both come out considerably ahead. Chen stuffed a glittering pile of coins into a paper bag, regretting his lack of pockets.

They found a small table in the large hall, nearly empty now. Chen talked about prospecting, something which he rarely allowed himself to do. He hardly knew any other way of life. His father had died when he was a baby, and of his mother he knew nothing. He had been left in the care of his father's partner, Inman, who had initiated him into the vast silences of space.

He was still afraid of space. He knew it so intimately. He had married it, it seemed, but he could never take it casually, nor had he ever come close to a gut-level understanding, an accord with the unconquerable emptiness between the suns.

Alsar sat close beside him, their arms lightly touching. She liked him. He was sentimental. She had seen so little of that lately. For En'varid, sentiment was a tool. Others carried around their self-sufficient supply of pity. But Chen seemed to toss on a sea, like a sailor afloat on his emotions.

"Alsar, could we go someplace where it's more private? Perhaps to the garden."

"No, I'd be seen leaving, and then En'varid would have many questions." She thought a moment. "Perhaps we could go upstairs, though. There is a fine library there, and I doubt En'varid will be reading tonight."

He followed her to a small door behind the pit where the darkened sandsnake lay, its amorphous carcass blending into the shadows of the sand. Alsar spoke softly to the door, and it slid silently open. They mounted a spiral staircase of wood with a waving gray grain. A deep carpet swallowed the sound of their ascent.

At the top of the stairs there was a broad, low hallway of the same wood. They passed one door to their right and another to the left, coming to a large double door at the opposite end of the hall.

"This is the library," Alsar whispered. She pushed the door softly ajar and slid inside, with Chen close behind her.

The cozy book-lined room was dimly lit by a blazing fire in a white marble fireplace, cut off from their view by a tight semicircle of five puffy leather chairs. A tall man leaned against the mantelpiece facing them. His face was in shadow, but Chen recognized him by his stance.

"Well," En'varid said casually, "Alsar. And who is this? A friend?"

From the leather chairs, five faces turned to look at them. Curious, self-assured men who did not spend time in idle speculation, but demanded to know. Their inelastic bodies stiffly shifted.

Alsar looked quickly at Chen, with an apology in her eyes. "I am sorry to disturb you, Lord En'varid. This is Chen. He is a friend of mine."

"Oh, yes? Bring him here in the light where I can see him, will you?" En'varid ordered peremptorily.

Chen squeezed between two chairs and faced the tall man. In his hand he still carried the paper bag containing the six hundred pieces he had won on the push-pull machines. Alsar remained by the door, which she had left ajar.

En'varid glanced curiously at the bag. "Yes, I remember your face. You look quite different without that ratty liner you space drifters affect." He turned to Alsar, a paternal tone creeping into his voice. "My dear, with all the rich and famous acquaintances I have introduced to you, must you drag such petty company as this grubbing prospector through my quarters?"

Chen reddened. En'varid smiled condescendingly. "I am afraid I must ask you to leave. But before you go, would you be so kind as to satisfy my curiosity as to what you are carrying in that brown paper bag? Are you perhaps taking home some of the fine *hors d'oeuvres* they are serving downstairs?" There was a slight titter from the five men behind Chen.

The prospector felt a surge of adrenaline pounding at his temples. Don't move, he told himself, give yourself a moment to calm down. "Nice to have made your acquaintance. I believe I know the way out." Chen wished he were a little better at repartee. He wished he could knock the asshole right into his fancy fireplace, but he knew it would take less of an excuse than that to give En'varid an opportunity to have him thrown in confinement, his ship confiscated.

He turned and walked out, stepping hard on the foot of one of the stolid men in the overstuffed chairs, who winced and looked baleful.

As he came up to Alsar, En'varid said, "She will stay." Alsar leaned close to him, brushing her nose lightly against his cheek. "I'm sorry, Chen," she whispered. Her eyes were drawn like bows.

She pushed the door shut behind him. There was a small click, and he was alone in the hall. He stared for a moment at the double doors, as if reconsidering, then walked rapidly away.

He made his way back to his stuffy cabin through a jabbering crowd and collapsed on the bed. As Chen fell asleep, thinking of the woman, Inman seemed to be always at his elbow, and Alsar stared at him with dreamy eyes of empty space.

Chapter Four

Chen woke instantly from a deep sleep.

"Wake up, damnit, wake up, you." Someone was shaking him roughly by the shoulder. His eyes tried to focus on the crumpled pillow. A dull somber light filled the room. The man shook him roughly again.

He was fully awake now. "Huh, what is it? What's that?" His voice was slurred with sleep. His hand groped under the pillow for the cold metal butt of his pistol. He crooked an arm under him and pushed off to the side, coming to his knees and covering the man with the pistol in one fluid motion.

It was then that he noticed the man was not alone. Two ship's crewmen with leveled rifles were posted at his door.

Chen put down the gun. "I'm sorry," he said.

"I am Commander Frederick Proun, serving as chief security officer on board this ship. Are you Chen?"

"Yes."

"And you are the registered owner and pilot of a Durry-Sundial surveyor, DS-48?"

"Yes, I am. Listen, is there anything wrong with my ship?" Chen looked at the armed crewmen doubtfully. You don't customarily bring along an armed guard to tell a pilot his ship has sprung an L-tube and is leaking radiation, or some such thing.

The officer smiled tightly. His hand flitted nervously to the rumpled cover of the bed, which he pulled taut.

"You are under arrest for the murder of Lord En'varid, secretary to the Herald of Arcturus. Now, will you kindly give me that gun and accompany me to see the captain?"

Chen flushed and then went pale. In a daze, he extended his handgun butt-first toward the officer. He slipped on his worn liner and followed the stiff little commander out of his compartment. Whispers and curious stares followed their procession toward the skin of the ship, where the command blister was located. The commander was almost swaggering, Chen trailing slightly behind, his mind and face a blank, the two guards bringing up the rear.

The light hurt Chen's eyes. He could not imagine En'varid dead. The night before, Chen had felt an enormous malicious vitality looming in the nobleman. He had almost expected En'varid to cast a shadow over the fire. No, perhaps this was just a trick of En'varid's, a hoax, but Chen didn't see how. . . .

Commander Proun preceded him into a low-ceilinged room that was even brighter than the corridor. The officer held the door for Chen. A blast of cold air swept out.

The room was totally white: walls, floor, and ceiling all smoothly tiled. There was a row of seven large tables, waist-high. To the far right the naked body of En'varid was laid out on its stomach.

A man in white was talking in a low precise voice to the captain, who bent attentively over the body. "Extremely close range, probably pushed right into his ribs right below the left shoulderblade. Caused his heart to freeze up in tetanic shock. Glycogen level of the liver shows he was taken by complete surprise."

Chen walked up to the table. The doctor and the captain looked up, startled, noticing him for the first time. Where the doctor had pointed was a slight sprinkling of fine white powder, like talc. En'varid's flesh was a dead white, except for the yellowish-orange soles of his feet. They had neglected to close his eyes.

The captain observed Chen curiously. He straightened his round cap on his bristling shock of hair and asked bluntly, "Did you kill this man?"

"No. Why should I want to kill him? I hardly even knew him."

"You saw him last night, didn't you?"

"Yes, briefly."

"And what did you talk about?"

"We didn't. He ordered me out of his quarters."

"And?"

"And I left," Chen said. "That's all. I went back to my cabin and fell asleep."

"When was that?"

"I don't remember. Around ten, I guess."

"Ten o'clock in the evening? Isn't that a bit early?"

"I was tired." Chen couldn't take his eyes off the body. It looked smaller now. He had not seen many dead men.

"Lord En'varid's body was found in your surveyor."

Chen groaned to himself in silent fury. His ship! He pictured the body sprawled in the dim blue light of the cabin. And then the men breaking in, ransacking the ship for evidence, bringing in floodlights, performing their arcane detective rituals on the virgin body of his new surveyor. Would he ever get to fly her again? If only he were floating in the black total silence a light-year away.

"I don't know anything about it," he finally managed to say lamely.

"As you can see, En'varid was killed with a stungun at close range." The captain pressed him. "Is that yours?" he asked, nodding to the gun that Commander Proun held loosely in his left hand.

"He pulled it on me, sir, when I woke him up!" Proun volunteered. "He looks like the one to me."

"Listen, Captain. Someone is trying to throw you on a false trail. I didn't kill En'varid!"

"Of course, there are tests for determining the truth of your assertion. Would you willingly submit to Truthtell?"

"Yes, certainly. The sooner we get this cleared up, the better."

The captain smiled obligingly. "I'm afraid that will have to wait till we reach Arcturus, as we don't have any personnel on this ship qualified to administer the drug. In any case, the proper Arcturian authorities will wish to examine you themselves." He turned to Proun. "Commander, place this man in confinement for the duration of the voyage."

"Confinement" was a small featureless cell with a hard cot, a sink, and a toilet with no seat. The floor was bare steel and cold. The door had a small one-way mirror set at eye-level. It was the first prison cell Chen had ever been in. It was just as he had imagined it. The novelty wore off in ten minutes. He spent the first day alone.

By midafternoon the lack of breakfast was beginning to tell. Anxiety curdled his stomach. No use in worrying, he reassured himself. They'll soon find out the truth. It would have been a monotonous cruise anyway.

He couldn't sleep. He tossed on the hard bunk for six hours before he fell into a fitful sleep, waking from languishing nightmares into a more real sense of oppression.

Around nine in the morning he jerked awake again at the faint hiss of the cell door sliding open.

"Good morning, friend. Sleep well? How do you like that bunk, huh? Really makes you want to confess your sins, doesn't it?" The thin, swarthy man laughed at his own joke as he laid a round aluminum tray bearing Chen's breakfast on the corner of the sink. He had a sharp nose with an indentation at the tip and a lousy set of teeth.

Chen sat up stiffly, throwing off his single blanket. He was relieved the night was finally over. He massaged his left foot, which tingled half-asleep.

"I like hard beds," Chen said. "They don't let you forget you're asleep."

His visitor chuckled obligingly. "Well, I'm sorry you

got left here so long. I was down in the after-galley—
I'm just a cook, really. Double as the jailer when
there's anyone here. Half the time they forget to tell
me. Haven't had anybody in here since three trips
back. There was a lady from Melmon, found her husband was stepping out on her. They were on one of
these 'Round the Galaxy' excursions, you know, retired. One night the lady slipped her husband some
kurlikew—a mighty powerful love potion, that is—and
a triple dose of 'quicker.' Pretty soon, he snuck off
down the way to see this teen-ager. Didn't make it
through the night, poor man," the jailer said solemnly,
then let out a loud, "Ha!" which exploded in the small
cell like a firecracker.

"My name's Jerson. What are you here for?"

"I'm Chen. I didn't do anything, just a stupid mistake."

"Well, what do they *think* you did?"

"They think I killed En'varid. Haven't you heard
about it yet?"

"That Arcturian in the lodge topside? Indeed I have.
Thought I'd hear your side first, though. I feel sorry for
you, fellow, when they get you to port. That's a nasty
nest of snakes you've stirred up. There were some hard
men here to look at you before breakfast."

"I didn't see anyone."

"They just wanted to look through the glass in the
door there, didn't ask to come in."

"Were they Arcturians?"

"I don't know, but I'd guess they were merchants—
the big sort, who buy and sell other merchants, not
goods. The no-nonsense sort."

Chen recalled the hard, disdainful faces of that tight
circle of men in the library. Perhaps one of those men
had been planning En'varid's murder when Chen
walked in. The scene in the library went through his
mind again and again as he stared mutely at the wall.
He would not forget those faces.

"You owe me two pieces, friend," the jailer finally
said.

"What?"

"For the breakfast."

"I have to pay you?" Chen asked stupidly.

"Why, of course," the jailer exclaimed. "I fix that food myself and cart it up here from the after-galley. Nobody, not even the captain's table, eats better than you."

Chen smiled ruefully.

"Besides, look, I'll let you out of your cell here," the jailer offered. "You can have the run of the anteroom and the other four cells—they're empty. I'm not worried about you escaping. There's nowhere to go, and besides, from the way those gentlemen were talking this morning, I'd consider myself in protective custody if I were you."

"Well, there's six hundred Arcturian mints I won last night in a paper bag in my cabin. You're welcome to that."

The jailer laughed. "No, they wouldn't be likely to overlook that in their investigation. May God commend me for my charity, but I'm not allowed to let you starve. Well, I have to go help get the lunch on. See you this evening."

The spry man hurried quickly out of the cell, leaving the door open. Chen heard him stride across the floor of the anteroom. There was the brief sound of conversation as the outer door opened, and then silence.

The anteroom was much larger than Chen's cell, with a polished wooden floor. It was in the shape of a regular pentagon, with a single door on each side. Four open doorways showed the interior of similar cells, and a fifth door of steel plate was closed tightly. Chen went immediately over to the closed door and pushed the button. The door stayed shut. No surprise. He searched the other cells and removed all the blankets to his own cell. There being nothing more to do, he sat down in the large anteroom with his back propped up against the wall beside the door to his cell.

For the first time since he had been taken into custody, his thoughts turned to the woman. What would she do now that her employer was dead? The same act that put him in jail had set her free. But they were both headed for Arcturus now, both of them captive to the same course.

Four days later she appeared early in the morning, alone in his doorway. He was sitting on his bunk playing solitaire. Alsar wore the same severe liner in which he had first seen her. Her eyes were somber, the fire in them quenched, or damped down.

"I would have come sooner, but Proun wouldn't allow it. I finally got through to your jailer, though." She sat down on the bunk beside him, slipping off her soft-soled shoes and tucking her feet under her.

"It was nice of you to come." There was a strained silence. "What happened?"

"They found En'varid murdered in your surveyor, about six in the morning. A tender went to investigate, because the hatch had been left open."

"Do you know who wanted to kill him?"

"En'varid had any number of powerful enemies. He stepped on a lot of feet to get where he was. Those men you saw in the library run five of the biggest cartels in the Dominions. They own planets. It might have been one of them. Or a Dominion councilman may have decided that En'varid was an intolerable thorn in their side, and had him extracted. Or it may have been a political rival—there are many Arcturians on board."

Chen looked askance at her. "I'm even in debt to my jailer. Well, this farce should come to an amusing end when we get to Arcturus."

"What do you mean?"

"Truthtell should convince them that I had nothing to do with En'varid's murder."

"Oh, Chen, you don't understand the danger. You will be assured of no fair trial on Arcturus. The truth is of secondary importance to them. Perhaps they will brand you a Dominion agent and use this murder as the excuse they have been waiting for to break with the Dominions. If not, they will probably still convict you.

Maybe one of En'varid's own deputies killed him. Maybe Darlan himself ordered it."

"They're not going to put me in prison for something I can prove I didn't do!" Chen shouted. Sweat broke out on his forehead.

Alsar sat with crossed legs, her shoulders sunken, her knee pressed against him.

"What will you do?" he asked. "The pilot's guild again?"

"Chen, be reasonable!" she cried. "I have to get you out of here. It's my fault."

"If you ask the jailer, he will let me out for a small sum. He has already offered. But where would I go then? They could find me anywhere on this ship as easily as coming to fetch me in my cell."

Alsar stared at him; her eyes were very bright.

"Listen," he said. "Maybe you could find out who really killed En'varid."

"And then?"

"Turn him over to the security officer."

"And if it turns out to be one of En'varid's associates? Or the security officer himself?"

"Alsar, please help me." He reached out and put his arms around her.

That evening the jailer sat on the end of his bunk filling him in on the daily rumors while Chen ate voraciously from an aluminum tray crowded with leftover delicacies from the captain's table.

"Most people make it out to be a jealous feud. Of course, some say that you were framed, too. Everyone's got his own pet theory. Some of the company at the captain's table seem to be quite shook up about it. I think these merchants just put through a big deal with En'varid before he got killed—they're clucking like birds who've just had their nest robbed."

"You'd make a good detective, Jerson. Who do you think killed him?"

"Well, friend, you've got too good an appetite to be the one. I'd say it was most likely one of En'varid's own party. I've been visiting Arcturus for twelve years on this run, and every time we dock, we hear some official was just done in by his own chief assistant. I'd look to see who steps into En'varid's place; that'll be your man. Oh, and I almost forgot. They've even got a witness up against you now."

"That's impossible!"

"Maybe." The jailer paused. Chen stared at him. "I think you know her, too."

Chen dropped a round ceramic plate, spilling a portion of shrimp in green sauce on the floor.

Jerson looked at the mess with a frown. "That lady that came to see you. Rumor says she's going to testify against you." He leaned closer. "They don't know she came to see you here. She came to me to ask to get in, confidential-like. Not playing both ends against the middle, is she?"

Chen stared mutely at the opposite wall till Jerson finally got up and left, taking the unfinished tray of food with him.

Chen had followed Alsar into this affair almost nonchalantly, and he had irrationally expected her to extricate him. Yet evidently someone had a powerful hold on her that she had not been willing to tell him about. The memory of the morning they passed together insistently tugged at his mind. He pushed it away. He kicked the ceramic plate across the floor. It clattered against the wall but refused to break.

Dragging a blanket behind him, Chen went out into the anteroom. He folded the blanket double and laid it on the floor in the middle of the room. He did the most difficult yoga asanas he knew for an hour, till his body was thoroughly exhausted and begged for rest.

In the penumbra of sleep, his mind still tossing and turning angrily, he thought he heard Alsar calling his name. He sat up abruptly. There was no one, just an echoing in his head. Yet he lay back down, more relieved than he had been for days, without knowing quite why, and was almost instantly asleep.

Chapter Five

The *Astrion* approached Kelos on a slightly curved trajectory and went into a tight orbit, completing a "fig-ure-six" landing made easier by the enormous mass and powerful gravity accelerators of the orbital city. The great ship settled into an expansive padded cradle with a thump that vibrated through the hull and walls. It was nestled among twelve other interstellar cruisers of various sizes ranged over a triangular landing field, ten miles on a side, that was one face of the dodecahedral shell of Kelos. The round cradle was sealed and the warehouse-sized dock pressurized. A convoy of men and machines wound out onto the floor of the room, encircling the huge smooth metal blister that was the intruding hull of the *Astrion*.

As the enormous hatches rumbled open, the walls of Chen's cell reverberated with the muted sound of pas-sengers making their last-minute preparations for leav-ing the ship. Some would catch the next passenger shuttle down to Arcturus, some a secondary cruiser to a neighboring backwater planet. Others would spend a few days visiting the free-floating city, where the atmo-sphere and entertainment were more cosmopolitan than on the surface of Arcturus.

In two hours the *Astrion* was more quiet than Chen had ever heard it. Even the familiar background mur-murings which he noticed only by their absence had faded slowly into an uneasy silence. There was only the whisper of the air duct to indicate that the ship was not dead, but sleeping. It wasn't till late in the ship's day—still morning, Kelos time—that Commander

Proun and the same two crewmen came to fetch him.
Proun brought along Chen's few personal possessions—minus his handgun and the winnings from
En'varid's lodge—in a white canvas bag with a draw-
string. The security officer carried the bag held a little
out from his body, waist-high, as if he had a rabbit by
the ears. Their walk wound through the empty ship and
from the dock down a long succession of deserted
cold-steel corridors marred and scratched by the passage of freight.

The walk was long. They kept him away from the
public thoroughfares and the bustling interior of the
city, where hostels, inns, casinos, cafés, brothels, and
souvenir shops were clustered in a three-dimensional
maze thronging with tourists, idle crewmen, pimps,
merchants, city workers, drifters, and the fancy rich up
from planetside on a night's outing. There Chen and
his escort would be another rare form of entertainment,
sure to draw a crowd of onlookers and hecklers. So
Proun led him through the scarred, ill-heated freight-
ways that were the ubiquitous capillaries of the commerce of Kelos.

They came finally to a small semicircular loading
platform. Four people waited beside the open door of a
ten-man passenger shuttle. They all turned to look as
Chen and his guards clattered down the corridor. There
was a pilot in a drab gray liner with military epaulets,
and two guards in police uniforms, one young and
handsome, the other pouchy-faced, with a cap adorned
with two silver stars and the emblem of the Rimhawk.

Alsar stood a little apart from the three men, and as
Chen turned his eyes on her, she averted her gaze, staring blankly at the smooth, curving hull of the shuttle.
She had not smiled, so Chen set his face in a tight une-
motional mask and did not look twice at her. Alsar was
evidently not under guard, so she could be here for
only one purpose—to incriminate him.

Proun turned over the bag and his prisoner to the
Arcturian officer with a few terse words—there was no
love lost between them. Proun favored Chen with a

curt nod of the head as he led his crewmen back, as if to say, "Now I wash my hands of the whole affair."

For a moment the little group stood motionless as the security officer and his two crewmen disappeared around a bend in the corridor. Then the older police officer took hold of Chen tightly behind the elbow and jerked him into the shuttle. As they were handcuffing him to a deeply cushioned seat between them, Chen saw Alsar stop the pilot as he made his way up the aisle behind them. She smiled at the pilot, and he bent his head to her.

She whispered in the pilot's ear, but Chen could hear plainly enough. "I wonder if I could sit up front with you? I'd rather not sit back here, with him. Surely you can understand?"

"Of course," the pilot eagerly consented. "I'd be delighted to have your company, if only for this short hop."

The older policeman looked doubtful as the pilot led Alsar into the control cabin and secured the thick door. He obviously didn't approve of the arrangement, but Chen imagined he had no jurisdiction over the pilot, and his witness surely couldn't slip away.

The three of them sat in the front row. There was nothing for Chen to look at but the bleak white bulkhead on which hung an official calendar surmounted by a stern three-D picture of the Herald. His arm was extended over a massive oaken desk, his shoulder cocked forward aggressively. There was no bland politician's smile. The eyebrows were drawn down over pale blue eyes, casting them into shadow. His hair was cut short and combed straight back. Darlan's face was not overbearing; it was insinuating. He could not have been picked out easily from a crowd, yet that cold face, bland and hard as a rock, would haunt Chen's dreams.

As Chen gazed fixedly at the picture, he felt the slight shocks as the Kelos controller shifted the small shuttle into position for takeoff. There was a surge, and they were catapulted out into space. Almost immediately, the pilot fired the forejets, and Chen judged from

the duration of the thrust that they were going straight
down, braking on their tailjets rather than spiraling
through three or four orbits to break their speed. Someone was in a real hurry to see him. The gravity drew
them down.

Less than a full minute later there was a sharp jerk,
and the ship seemed to slip to the side. Chen pushed
his wrists against the manacles that held them to the
arms of the chair. The older guard let out a surprised
grunt.

The ship righted itself instantly, but now there was a
subtle difference in the thrust, as Chen's trained pilot's
reflexes were quick to realize. They were making headway horizontally as they sank toward the face of the
planet, an extremely difficult maneuver that was not often attempted, as it was dangerous and unnecessary, for
the pilot could maneuver freely in space to the requisite
position before he commenced the descent.

The two guards exchanged worried glances, and the
officer pushed a button mounted in the arm of his
chair.

"Captain Ee'lom?" he queried.

"Nothing to worry about, gentlemen," Alsar's calm
voice came over the intercom. "Our number-three after-
jet cut out for some reason. Captain Ee'lom is checking
down the support systems now. Please do not disturb
us for the moment."

Chen tensed in his seat, hoping the guards would not
notice. The older guard wiped his forehead on his
sleeve. His companion stared ahead without expression.
Chen could tell that the incident had unnerved them a
bit, but they did not seem to be suspicious.

They had good reason to be. Chen knew that the
number-three jet had not cut out; instead, what they
had felt was a brief lapse of control—as if the controls
had changed hands. And then they had changed
course—only slightly, but at this altitude even a slight
course differential would bring them down half a conti-
nent away from their original target.

Alsar was kidnapping him.

Twenty minutes later they grounded lightly, belly-down on soft soil. Before Chen's guards had risen from their seats, Alsar poked her head from behind the door of the control cabin. She smiled at the younger guard, who was sitting nearest the aisle. "Could I have a word with you?"

The guard unstrapped himself and got up. As he approached her, Alsar leaned forward and cupped her hand to her mouth, as if to whisper something to the guard. He leaned forward to listen, and before she even touched him, collapsed on the floor in a heap.

"Oh, I think he's fainted!" she exclaimed. She bent over the prostrate man.

"Hold it!" The officer quickly rose from his seat, pulling his stungun from its cylindrical holster. He had to step over Chen's legs to get to the aisle, and as he brushed past with his eyes on the woman, Chen lashed out with his feet, sweeping the guard's legs out from under him, spilling him into the aisle. Chen aimed a kick at the back of his neck, but the guard rolled to the side, seeking to rise, and Chen's blow glanced off his shoulder. Before he could kick the man again, Alsar had straightened up, the other guard's gun in her hand. She sent a charge into the struggling officer, and he collapsed heavily on the floor, letting the gun roll from his fist.

Alsar rummaged through the officer's pockets till she came up with the key to Chen's manacles. As she leaned over him to undo his wrist-cuffs, he bent forward and kissed her on the ear.

She smiled and pushed back a strand of hair. "That wasn't easy. Thanks for the help." She sprung the second cuff. "Hurry now."

She led him to the forward hatch. It was a short distance to the ground. She jumped and took off running, with Chen a short distance behind her.

He caught up with her as she topped the rise. She halted for a moment. He was breathing in short hard gasps, but Alsar didn't look winded. Her nostrils were flared.

Below them, in a small hollow, the ship lay across a small stream, surrounded by a circle of charred grass, wreathed in thin wisps of smoke and steam.

"Come on, no time." She pulled his hand, and he started down the other side of the hill behind her, his feet digging deep into the sandy loam. Through the sparse pines he could see a small settlement of not more than fifty wooden buildings. Beyond the town was a broad expanse of blue. Three small sailing ships were tilting their white sails in the wind.

They stopped behind a hedge that screened them from a row of modest pine-board cottages. Chen could hear faint music from the other side of the small resort community. The birds were singing very loud.

"What now?" he asked.

"Got to steal a flitter. You stay here. You look too conspicuous. I'll be back in a minute."

Alsar disappeared around the hedge. In little more than a minute she was back, skimming silently over the bush, to hover a foot over the ground in a new, red, open-air flitter. Chen hopped in beside her, and she banked up and back at full acceleration, shooting up over the town and out to sea. She headed west toward the sun, which was low in the sky, following the coast-line.

When they had put the sleepy town safely out of sight behind them, Alsar turned inland, following the twisting course of a small stream that lay at the bottom of a steep ravine. Chen found himself gripping the side of the door with all the force he could muster. Several times it seemed they were about to rake the side of the ravine with the whirling blades. Alsar was winding up the stream at breakneck speed. Before Chen had quite recovered from one close brush with death, they were running full-tilt at another obstacle. Alsar was flying with total concentration, not daring to glance at him for an instant, twisting the spongy jumpstick with desperation at every turn or rise.

About ten miles inland they came on a broad valley, which, Chen figured, judging by the sun, ran more or less parallel to the coastline. They turned and headed east, back the way they had come. They were going even faster now, but the path was clear. They followed open meadows, flushing small game from the tall yellow grass now and then.

"We're making a slight detour to throw them off our track," Alsar shouted through the tearing wind.

Chen leaned closer, careful not to interfere with her steering. "It's going to get dark soon," he shouted.

"Be there soon."

He didn't bother to ask where. They soon came to the end of the broad grass valley and passed out between two smooth hills. They were now skimming over a great coniferous forest. An even carpet of huge trees coated the land as far as Chen could see in every direction, their branches swaying the slipstream as they whirred past, like water in the wake of a boat.

Alsar kept on due east. She was scanning the forest from north to south. Then Chen saw what she was looking for, a scar in the foliage, another stream bed cut deep into the sandstone. She dropped down into the shadow of the ravine and headed once more for the sea, forced to cut her speed now, for the bed of this stream was narrower than the other, and it was getting darker.

The stream debouched onto a broad sandy beach backed by towering sandstone cliffs. Alsar ditched the flitter in the ocean near the mouth of the stream, where the undercurrent would carry it into deeper water. It sank, with the rotoblades pulling it upside-down to the bottom, leaving a trail of bubbles. Towing their bundled-up liners, they swam easily ashore in the tepid water.

The cliffs behind the beach were more than a hundred feet high. In many places the storm-driven water had undercut them, and the broad beach was littered with enormous piles of rubble that reached almost to the water, the tall cliffs showing bright yellow where they had been freshly excised.

They walked by the edge of the water, where the

beach had been scoured of rubble but was frequently obstructed by heaps of blue seaweed. The fresh wind and burning blue sun dried their bodies quickly, leaving little tracks of salt on their skin. Alsar held his hand. The water washed away their footprints. They were still headed east; their shadows stretched out long before them.

Two miles down the beach, they came to an exceptionally large swath of rubble that reached from near the top of the cliffs out into the ocean like a breakwater.

"We'll go up here." Chen looked doubtfully at the steep, jumbled slope. Some of the blocks were as big as a house. They paused to wash the sand off their feet before donning their liners and soft shoes.

Once more it was necessary to hurry. The sun was on the horizon, and the air promised to turn as cold as it had been hot while the blue sun was blazing down on their backs. They had to climb side-by-side so as not to dislodge rocks on each other. Twice they started landslides that shook the whole slope. Near the top, the talus was almost vertical, and they had to zigzag to keep their footing.

Their bruised ankles threatening to give way, they finally flopped down on the ragged tufts of brownish grass that held down the soil of the bluff. They had been in constant motion for almost two hours, and Chen estimated they must have covered more than a hundred miles, by flitter, swimming, on foot, and lastly clambering on all fours up the talus.

Alsar lay on her back, her ribcage rising and falling heavily, seeking to recharge her wrung-out muscles with oxygen. She looked at Chen through eyes that were slightly glazed. He knelt, surveying the coastline and the horizon for any movement. A chilly breeze was rising up the slope, smelling of salt and rotting seaweed. The conifers were gathering darkness under their thick branches. The treetops, as well as a few icy dots of cloud hung high in the stratosphere, were catching the last golden rays of the sun, already set.

"Arcturus is very nice," Chen said when he had caught his breath, "right here and now, anyway. Where are we?"

"On the shores of the South Polar Sea, about the thirtieth parallel. Across this sea—about five thousand miles on a major arc—is the administrative capital, Piedsplat, where they intended to take us."

"Is this area populated?"

"The nearest town is the one from which we stole the flitter, about seventy-five miles from here. This is a commercial forest. These are Earth cedars planted more than a century ago. They won't be harvested for another century or so. We're not likely to run into anyone, or anything—Arcturian wildlife prefers it's natural habitat."

Chen looked around again. This was one of the few times in his life he could recall that there was not a single piece of machinery, no flat wall, or artificial light to be seen. He felt more exposed than he ever had floating in a surveyor light-years from the nearest life, bottled up in his ship like a fish in an aquarium.

"Is this your favorite picnic ground or something?" It seemed almost like a park to him, too peaceful to be wild.

"Not mine. Come on. We've just a short way to go yet."

They set off at a more leisurely pace, winding between the cedars. The floor of the forest was spongy, sparsely carpeted with grass, rising in a gentle slope away from the bluff. Alsar walked quietly, sunk in thought as if she were taking a stroll in the open air, hoping to solve some problem which had been cooped up in her mind for days.

Chen tried to guess where they were headed. Maybe a campsite she knew of, or a cottage. They couldn't stay out in the open indefinitely. The thermostats in their liners would keep them warm for one night perhaps, but after that the microcells would be drained and they would suffer from the exposure. They had no food or water. Chen could hardly see the ground now, but Alsar forged on without slackening her pace.

They came to an outcrop of shiny metamorphic rock that rose like a wall, blocking the forest. It was a dark greenish shade, and brittle. Probably serpentine, Chen thought, poor man's jade. Alsar led him first to the right, and then to the left, till she found a place where they could ascend the jagged wall. Chen had difficulty following her trail. He bruised his knees, and then cut his left hand on a sharp protrusion. In places, the face of the rock felt smooth, as if the rock had been chiseled away to make the passage easier. They climbed gradually up to a level with the tops of the cedars. There was a ledge there which held enough topsoil to cradle a full-size tree, standing alone on the side of the slope. Its roots had insinuated deep feelers into the surrounding rock, crumbling it. At the surface the roots were exposed, giving the tree the appearance of having been uprooted at one time in its history, and then set down again.

"Home at last," Alsar said when they both stood in the deep night-shade of the tree. She ducked her head and disappeared into a low cleft in the trunk, which Chen could barely make out in the darkness. Feeling his way cautiously, he followed. Inside the trunk was a level dirt floor, and Chen, feeling above his head with his hand, found he could safely stand erect.

Alsar's hand came out of the darkness and clasped his. "Watch. There are stairs. Fifteen steps to the bottom."

Chen counted them. Then he could feel a level concrete floor under his feet. What was all the mystery?

Alsar turned on the light, revealing a windowless metal door set in the natural stone and above the door, a carved bas-relief of a Rimhawk with television lenses set in the eyes. Alsar said a word, and the door rolled silently back.

More steps led down onto the floor of an airy natural cave with a domed ceiling caused by a bubble of gas trapped in the molten rock. Veins of red, orange, yellow, and blue were woven into the shiny greenish schist. The floor of the cavern had been leveled and a floor of well-waxed cedar laid down, here and there carpeted with the long-haired pelts of big game. The room was divided into three areas by movable cloth screens just over six feet high. In one corner a servo had been set into the rock beside a ponderous oaken dining table. Two chairs were pushed back from the table, and a disarray of dirty plates and rotting food were still spread over it. In another section there was a large canopied bed and a chest of drawers. The largest section of the chamber contained a large boxlike metal desk, two leather chairs, and a long sofa drawn up facing a row of closed metal shutters.

Alsar watched Chen quickly surveying the room. "There's no one here," she said. "Don't worry. We won't be disturbed. This belonged to En'varid. . . ."

Chen felt like a mouse that has just been introduced to a mousetrap.

"It was his private hideaway. Not even his wife knew its location. He owned all this forest for a hundred miles in any direction."

"How did . . . ?" Chen started to ask. He stopped. He had often wondered about the relationship between Alsar and En'varid. How had she known about this place? Had she merely flown him here? But the dinner table was set for two.

"There are many things which I have put off explaining to you, Chen." She put her arms around him and looked him directly in the eyes. "You have been drifting along on the surface of a current that runs very deep. Admittedly, I was the siren that lured you in, but I did not create the sea or the current. I will explain, but let's eat first."

Chapter Six

Chen had never eaten a better meal. The servo dished them up three salads, a course of pungent fish, a small game hen, spineless artichokes with mayonnaise, and plum pie. He drank almost a full liter of dark red claret that tasted like grape juice. Afterward he sprawled out on the deep cushions of the brocade sofa. Alsar turned out the lights and opened the steel shutters which ran along one wall, revealing a broad balcony roofed over by a protrusion of serpentine. With his head propped up against an arm of the sofa, Chen looked out over the treetops to the distant sea, where he could barely make out a lacy pattern of phosphorescence which lay on the crests of the incoming waves. The servo hummed faintly as it washed the dishes and reduced their leftovers to dust.

Chen was beginning to feel pangs of indigestion. His stomach hurt every time he moved, so he tried to lie still and let the distant sea soothe him. But his calm was undermined by nervous agitation. He wanted to pace up and down, to run, to scream, to do anything to relieve it. He was being poked and prodded by despair. Alsar was right—he had just been drifting, all along. At first he had struggled with the situation, seeking to define it, come to grips. But three weeks on the *Astrion* had brought him no mental foothold, only self-pity for the grievous stroke of fate which had smashed his hopes, stolen his ship, and now cast him adrift under an alien sun. He was clinging to the hard simple fact of his own innocence like a log in a storm-driven sea, trying to hold his head above the water in a hurricane of political and economic conflict which he couldn't fathom, waiting for the dawn. If what Alsar had just told him was right, the whole fabric of commerce and communication that held the Dominions together was about to rip asunder under the combined pressure of Arcturus and her mercantile allies. The huge cartels would carve up the Dominions into convenient monopolies, with Arcturus reigning supreme over a third of the colonies, including Earth. All over the galaxy men and women were being swept up in the intrigue, some in loyalty, some out of fear, out of greed, out of selfishness. But Chen felt he did not belong in this interstellar drama. He was just out in the open when the storm blew by. It might have just missed him, but it hadn't.

He was tormented by a longing to be far away, ransacking some backwater of space, he and his ship, two jewels of life, the one biochemical, the other mechanical. Ever since he was a child, Chen had always thought people were nothing more than elaborate machines, each with his own motivation, his course in space, each with his own ego-centered gravity. He had careened on by person after person, and never had anyone pulled him in, till this woman.

His train of thought always came back to the same point. That memory of Alsar and the crystal flower, alone in the garden, pricked him like the unseen thorn on a rose. It was fitting he should have met her there in the garden. The flower and she were a pair of enigmas.

It was the crystal flower that had led him out here to this patch of space in the first place. The mysterious gem that came from nowhere, that a laser couldn't cut. ... Yes, they had tried in vain to break a piece off that flower. Tried in vain, but in a leg pocket of his liner, Chen carried a piece. It was a small crystalline thorn about two inches long, an inch across at the base, and clear as a diamond. It had not come off the flower on the *Astrion*—Chen had examined it well—but it was made of the same stuff.

Inman had given the crystal to him. It was his single legacy, the only thing he had salvaged from the ship-

wreck of his life. Chen knew it was important to the
old man. It was his talisman, a charm which he held in
awe and would not speak of. The crystal reminded Inman of the terrors of the garden in which these crystal
flowers grew. With this tangible proof of its existence,
Chen had set out to find that garden. He felt he owed
that to Inman. He could feel the slender shape of ada-
mantine crystal against his thigh through the material
of his liner. It was a constant reminder.

"Are you sorry I brought you here?"

Chen looked up. Alsar had been studying the expression on his face.

"No. Of course not. You saved my life, probably.
From what you told me over dinner about the political
situation, I imagine they would have executed me as a
most convenient scapegoat."

Alsar perched on an arm of the sofa, nervously
erect. "I thought perhaps you wouldn't understand. I
would not try to conceal from you the fact that you
have just exchanged one prison for another."

She was right, Chen thought. He had been skirting
around that realization all evening, trying to avoid it.
Not only this palatial hideaway, but the whole planet
was his prison. He couldn't even see the sky from here;
it was cut off by the rocky ledge that overhung the balcony.

"Alsar, how could you doubt that I would understand why you did this, and be grateful? You risked
your life for me."

Alsar studied her hands. She looked out to the sea.
Finally she said. "No, Chen. It was you who risked
your life for me. I thought it would be easier for me to
rescue you than it would for you to rescue me."

"What? I don't understand."

"I killed En'varid," she said flatly.

Chen sprang to his feet, barely conscious of the tearing pain in his stomach. "You framed me! You took
him to my ship! You sent them after me!"

"But you were the only one. So defenseless, so obvi-
ous. Had I tried to pin the blame on someone else, they

would have investigated further. They would have found me out. I would have been taken, and you wouldn't have had a chance to save me!" Her voice sank slowly to a dead calm. "I don't know what you must think of me now. But I almost . . ." She stopped, but then went on remorselessly, to get it over with. "I have explained much of what is happening in this little corner of the galaxy to you. But there is more, more that I absolutely cannot tell you now. I *must* be free. There is more at stake than my own skin, or I would never have done it. Please trust me!"

Chen stood wobbling on his feet. His stomach was turning over violently, and he was trying to concentrate on her, a flood of contradictory emotions washing over him: anger, regret, resentment, mixed with a certain affection and even sympathy for Alsar. Then it all seemed to coagulate into one great nauseous lump surging up into his throat, and before he quite knew what he was doing, he found himself kneeling on the edge of the balcony, spewing his supper into the darkness below.

The wind blew against the sweat on his face, making it feel like a cold mask.

Drained of all emotion, he was hardly conscious of Alsar helping him to bed. Lying still, careful not to jiggle the cold shards of his stomach, he saw her face framed in the darkness. He didn't know whether his eyes were open or not. Her eyes were boring into him; he was expanding into them. Each golden fleck became a sun, and Chen—who had learned to know the stars before he could read—was lost. He could pick out no pattern he knew, turning madly in all directions, till out of the darkness rushed the slate-gray eyes of Inman. Inman, mottled skin pulled taut over his cheekbones, and a leer on his face. Chen remembered it well—that leer that Inman would put on when he was contemplating with satisfaction some backside of space no man had ever seen before. And he would turn to Chen and say, "That old witch, space, will come at you with arms wide open, but don't be fooled. When you lurch for

her, you'll find yourself falling free, and not a friendly
star in sight, just locked in cold. . . ."

The morning light washed away a dreamless sleep,
and he awoke to the nightmare memory of the previous
night. Chen sprang out of the big double bed and
looked around for his clothes.

He was alone.

His liner was crumpled on the floor. As he put it on,
he studied the bed. Alsar had slept there too the night
before. The silence was oppressive. He looked into the
dining room. On the massive table there was a single
plate with a few crumbs and streaks of egg, a glass with
dregs of orange juice and nutritional yeast.

Chen looked around for a clock. Ten-twenty A.M. He
hadn't slept so late for a long time. The shutters were
still open, and a soft breeze blew in through the balcony. The sea twinkled in the distance. Chen sat down
heavily on the sofa.

"Shit," he said.

He found himself wishing she had stayed, in spite of
her monumental treachery. On the dining-room table
was a terse note. "I must leave, Chen. You will be safe
here. You have adequate food for three months. There
is a television. If I do not return by then, go west along
the beach to the nearest town. I'm sorry." No signature.

After having assured himself that the door was not
locked, Chen sat down to a large breakfast. He had a
good appetite, and the food did not make him sick as
before. He grinned to himself at the thought of staying
there for three months, watching on the video as the
Empire of Man came apart at the seams. No, at last he
was free to make his own path. Apparently Alsar
couldn't take it upon her conscience to be his jailer,
even though she'd had him thrown in jail in the first
place . . . and then risked her life to get him out. And,
anyhow, what if she didn't come back? The thought of
her body laid out on an antiseptic slab like En'varid
brought a twinge of the previous night's nausea back to
him.

And what if she *did* come back? He wouldn't be here. This was good-bye.

From the servo he got enough fruit juice to fill two empty wine bottles. He wrapped up six sandwiches and a pound of cheese in cloth napkins. Ripping the kapok out of a fur pillow, he made himself a serviceable rucksack. He bound a warm light blanket with a length of electrical cord and tucked a steak knife into a leg pocket. En'varid's large desk was a temptation, but it was sealed shut, and Chen knew he would be wasting his time trying to open it. He imagined the first thing he would find would be a large photo of Alsar and En'varid, arm-in-arm.

The air circulated freely in the lofty chamber, filling it with motion. In another moment he was standing in the open air before the forked roots of the tortured cedar. The wind seemed to cleanse him of a host of unidentifiable anxieties. He felt like he was going on an impromptu picnic. A leisurely stroll down the beach should get him to the nearest town in three or four days. When he got there, he would have to play it by ear.

There were two paths down off the face of the rock. They had come up from the right, so Chen started down to the left. This path ended shortly at a steel door camouflaged to blend in with the rock. The escarpment was nearly vertical, and Chen could make out the faint line of a larger door of rock. It was probably a garage, but he couldn't open the voice lock. Alsar would have taken the flitter anyway, if there had been one. He turned back past the gnarled cedar and down into the forest.

A stroll through the quiet forest brought him quickly to the edge of the sandstone cliffs. He slid down the talus in a barrage of dislodged rust-yellow rocks. Skirting the piles of seaweed, he made his way along the edge of the sea, walking barefoot in the warm water.

When he came to the first river—where they had ditched the flitter—he walked upstream a bit and swam across, sidestroking with his sack and bedroll held awkwardly above the water. A few miles down the beach there was another stream, and shortly, another. After he had forded the fourth, he realized that his estimate of the distance he could travel in one day must be considerably revised. Already he had inadvertently dropped the bedroll into the water, but luckily the knapsack had proved water-resistant. The sandwiches were a bit soggy, but edible. His initial elation turned quickly to boredom, and he plodded on, squishing the sand through his blistered toes, his eyes focused on the pale sand immediately in front of him.

He didn't notice the small blue flitter. It picked up his trail in the early afternoon, following him at a distance, hidden behind the tops of the cedars that backed the beach. The three men inside watched impatiently as their quarry crept like a snail up the beach. They were waiting for him to go to ground.

When the sun dropped below the horizon, the stars came out so suddenly it seemed as if they had been switched on, and the waves glowed. Chen walked back to the cliffs, obscuring his footprints as best he could. At the base of the cliffs it was pitch dark. He felt along the wall till he came upon a pocket cut into the soft stone. It was deep and shallow. He scooped out a quantity of sand, clearing a space large enough to stretch his legs out, piling the sand at the edge of the hole till he had practically walled himself off from the beach.

Stretched out in a cocoon of still-warm sand, he ate two of the sandwiches, chewing the small bites thoroughly to savor the last lingering taste of the dark bread and salty meat, then washed them down with a half-bottle of fruit juice.

His blanket was still wet, but the sand would keep him warm. He turned up the isotherm unit of his liner and felt his muscles unknot as a gentle warmth spread throughout his body. The incoming waves were small and silent. In the small arc of sky that Chen could see from his hole, a bright dot was passing overhead. Arcturus had no moon, just an orbital "alley" of half a dozen "free" cities, a chain of forts and research and industrial plants for weightless manufacturing. The dot passed out of sight. Chen was more fatigued than he had realized. Tomorrow every joint and limb would ache.

He was dreaming of horses, fleet, running silently on the sand. . . . There was the sound of voices. He woke. Silence, now. He wasn't sure if the voices were part of his dream, or if they had broken it. He rolled over cautiously and craned his head over the low mound of sand. To his left, three figures in dark cloaks were moving down the beach away from him, one at the edge of the water, one by the cliffs, and one between. They carried rifles. As the one in the middle turned his head, sweeping the expanse of beach with his sight, Chen could see he had a visor over his eyes. Chen ducked quickly back into his hole and hastily covered his body again with sand. Infrared snoopers. He was fortunate—they had missed him. Even though the liner was an almost perfect insulator, without the blanket of sand, the snooper would have picked him up. The man sweeping the base of the cliff must have passed close enough to reach out and touch him.

He waited ten minutes before he chanced another look. The beach was deserted. He let out a faint sigh of relief.

Down the beach were all outlines of sea, sand, and cliff merged into blackness, there was a blinding flash. A flare floated slowly down toward the beach, silhouetting the crouching figures of the men in cloaks that had just passed. They turned toward the cliff. Had they flushed someone? Chen shielded his eyes from the glare with his hand. A small black dot came flying down from the cliff to land beside the middle figure. Chen ducked, burying his face in the sand and plugging his ears. A piercing wail ripped the fabric of the air, filling the closed space of the dugout with a fine dust as the sonic blast pulverized the outermost layer of rock. Close by, a section of the cliff came thundering down.

In the deafened silence, even the waves were quiet.

Chen raised himself on his elbows. His head was throbbing hard enough to make him fear his eyeballs were loose in their sockets. Before the flare went out abruptly, he got a hazy view of three twisted figures lying on the beach.

Soon sounds of movement came to his tortured ears from down the beach. Chen hurriedly pushed sand up on his wall till there was barely a crack at the top. It was claustrophobic. His breath came harshly through his parted lips. He couldn't see out.

The sibilant sound of footsteps. A bright light stabbed through the crack, swept on, and came again to rest on Chen's hiding place.

"Boss, come here," someone called.

More footsteps. "Look. This sand's been piled here."

"Come out of there," another voice called.

Chen didn't answer.

"If you don't come out, we will be forced to use another grenade, and I imagine you are still gritting your teeth from the last one."

Chen shouldered his way out of the narrow hole. He was trying to feel anger so he wouldn't feel fear. As he straightened up, the light played full in his eyes, then moved down to search his cubbyhole, letting him see three men. There were two younger men, in their mid-twenties, and an older man with a turn-down mouth and a hairless, sunburned pate. They carried helmets in their hands. They were not the same three men that had passed him by earlier.

One of the younger men searched his cubbyhole, coming out with his wet bedroll and rucksack. The old man turned down his mouth another notch. "Search him."

They piled his possessions on the sand beside him: a box of matches, the stub of a candle, the steak knife, a pair of dry socks and thin elastic shoes, and the fragment of crystal that Inman had bequeathed him. That was all. They had cleaned him out on the *Astrion*.

The old man turned each object over in the bright

beam of his flashlight before replacing it in Chen's sack. He saved the crystal for last. He looked it over for a long time.

Chen could not restrain the urge to say something. "It's my good-luck charm."

The deep-sea eyes of the bald man demanded what else. He handed it back with a smile. "You'll need it."

He waited to see if Chen would say something. Then he added, "Allow me to introduce myself. I am Marcos Bosaven. Call me Boss. I am a representative—though not a public one—of the Dominions. Perhaps you have heard of me? No? It is safe to talk."

"Safe?" Chen asked blankly.

"Do you doubt my identity? Didn't they tell you about me?" Boss swung the beam of his own flashlight full on his face. The upward shadows gave him an inhuman look. "They must have told you about me. At any rate, they told me about *you*."

"Then perhaps you'd better tell me, too."

Boss flushed. "I don't enjoy that kind of sarcasm. You"—he stabbed Chen in the chest with his finger—"are a paid assassin, sent by Councilman Flur d'Hiver to dispose of a great threat to the peace of the Dominions—as he put it. You murdered Lord En'varid and escaped—I don't know how—with your skin intact. I have been instructed to find you and get you off this planet before you spark an incident." Boss paused, looking out over the lacy phosphorescence of the incoming waves. "My task would have been a lot easier if you had not botched things so badly already!"

"I don't know what you're talking about. I was just hiking down the beach. Now, come to think of it, I did pass a fellow this afternoon. He was going in the other direction. Maybe that's who you're after." Chen smiled lamely.

Boss took a folded square of paper from his hip pocket and passed it over to Chen without a word. Chen spread it out in the wavering light of the flashlight. A life-size, tri-D photo taken from his pilot's license was surmounted by the single crimson word, "AS-

SASSIN," in three-inch block print. Underneath the photo was Chen's name, a detailed physical description, and "$100,00 REWARD" in the same red capital letters.

"Come with me, eh?"

Chen followed the Dominion agent down the beach, with the two assistants bringing up the rear. They stopped by the huddled form of one of the other trio of men that had been hunting Chen. Bending over the man, Boss caught hold of his cowl and jerked it back. A thin trickle of blood ran from the corner of the man's mouth. The top of his face was obscured by the opaque nightvisor. Boss pulled this off too, revealing a face frozen in a nerve-gnashing grimace. A tight circlet bound his hair, and set in the middle of the circlet was the emblem of the Rimhawk.

The man let out a faint groan. Chen started.

Boss let the policeman's head fall to the sand and stood up. "He'll live. Won't remember a thing. Traumatic amnesia.

"If I had not stopped these men," Boss continued, "they would have made it very unpleasant for you. You may have wished *you* could forget everything. Now, Chen, if you want to go on covering up, I'm not going to beat it out of you. There's nothing I really have to know. I'm just supposed to get you off the planet before you start a war."

They turned back down the beach, with Boss talking half to Chen, half to himself, firing off rapid phrases. "Those fatheads on Earth are always going off half-cocked, sending men into my territory without warning me. When they've mucked it up beyond repair, they come after me; good old Boss is supposed to patch it up, or face the consequences. They didn't tell me about this one, either—don't want to trust me with too much information. Listen, Chen, you got caught with your pants down, and I saved your ass, so I expect some co-operation from you!"

"All right. My name is Chen. But I am not a paid assassin. I'm a prospector. I was on the *Astrion*. I didn't kill En'varid. I was framed. Have you got some Truthtell? I'll prove it!"

Boss looked at him dubiously. "Well, cover or no cover, I'll have to get you out of here." He turned down the beach. "You're a hot potato, Chen."

Chapter Seven

It was a tedious seven-hour journey to Piedsplat. They flew as high and fast as their battered Beesun sedan would go, the blades thrushing the thin air desperately. The bubble frosted up, and Chen could see nothing below. The flight passed in silence.

As they approached the capital, they dropped low, skipping over the waves. The froth washed the bubble, clearing their view. The city glittered still at two in the morning under a soft cloud of light reflected off the sky and the sea. On the maze of small islands that shielded the harbor from the open sea, a tall ring of white towers rose above the trees, throwing bright fingers of light into the bay and out to sea. They turned into a narrow canal shadowed by tall overhanging trees. The trees sent down a dark shower of leaves in the wake of their passage; the harbor opened before them.

They dropped lightly into the midst of a thicket of flitters, hydrofoils, skimmers, and primitive sailing ships that were moored together on a floating jetty. There were several people wandering about, but none remarked Chen's pale, drawn face. The three men hemmed him in, talking excitedly about the torch-fishing. They clambered aboard another, smaller, rakish flitter. It was just a short hop to a large two-masted schooner that was anchored in a secluded pocket of the harbor.

Chen preceded them awkwardly up a rope ladder to the deck. Before he had a good look at the ship, Boss led him down below. As the interior lights came on, Chen had the impression of being inside a well-cared-for toy. There was no steel in sight, just brass, glass, and a mélange of different shades and textures of wood. It had a functional simplicity that was the exact opposite of the baroque elegance of En'varid's lodge on the *Astrion*. Four straight chairs were drawn up to a felt-covered table in the middle of the room. A slightly sagging rattan couch leaned against one wall, beside a hat-rack with several blue-black sailors' caps. Boss's assistants each took a cap. They had the name "Lethe" stitched across the crown.

Boss held one out. "Ever played sailor before, Chen?"

"No."

As he didn't reach for the cap, Boss thumped it on his head. "Well, I don't think you'll find it intolerable for the time being." He turned to the man on Chen's right, a young man with a tanned face, unwrinkled except for the crow's feet behind the eyes. "John, take Chen to his bunk and find him some decent clothes. I am going ashore to make some inquiries. I hope you sleep soundly, Chen. The motion of the sea is very quieting."

The next day was one of those sultry days that seem so out of place in the fall. A mass of black-bottomed clouds hung over the harbor. The air was charged with static electricity. John invited Chen out on the deck to show him the ropes, guys, spindles, and pulleys which enabled one man to sail the two-masted schooner with difficulty, or two men with ease. Boss and the other man were nowhere to be seen, and the flitter was no longer tied up at the side of the boat. They sat with their backs to a hatch cover, looking over the bay to the domes and spires of Piedsplat.

John ran a yard of smooth line through his fingers. He was showing Chen some of the complex but functional knots they used in the rigging. For a time Chen showed interest. As a boy, he had passed long afternoons in deep space learning the intricate knot-writing of Adelin IV. But Chen's eyes kept darting over the harbor uneasily. He wondered idly where Alsar could be. Perhaps in one of those windowless buildings that rose like sun-bleached bones above the blue-green line of shrubs and trees.

Strangely, he didn't feel angry for what she had done to him. A curiosity impelled him to find her once again. He wanted to know more about her. He would swim for it that night, he decided. If he could make it to the jetty before his absence was detected and steal a flitter . . .

John stopped midway through his explanation of a "double-slung tripe," realizing he no longer had Chen's attention. He pointed to the sprawling city. "Wish you were there?"

"Oh, no. I was just thinking what a lovely harbor this is. Too bad I don't get a chance to vacation dirtside more often."

"Well, if you want to make a break, now's probably your best chance. Ja'in and the Boss have gone into town to check you out. And I can't risk chasing you about the harbor in broad daylight. Too conspicuous." He paused, waiting for a reaction. "Of course, some Arkie would probably fish you out of the harbor and turn you in for the reward. After that, no telling what might happen. You could bang off a nice little war, and get yourself decomposed in the process. We could have kept you confined below, but Boss didn't want you to feel restrained. If you're really Flur d'Hiver's man, he can't risk mishandling you. I hope you see it's in your own interest to stay on this boat."

Chen realized that what John had said was true. To escape now would be absurdly rash, for he did want off the planet, and they could get him off. But he wanted another chance with Alsar too. There was more mystery to her, he sensed, than all these police and politics.

He shook his head and stood up brusquely. "I'm going inside," he announced. John looked up. Chen could see something, almost fear, in his eyes. To him I must be a walking, ticking time bomb, Chen thought, liable to go off any moment now. For an instant he felt respect for John's patient fear, while the entire inhabited galaxy turned in its sleep, forever ignorant.

He turned and went back inside the empty ship.

John and Ja'in came back to the small four-berth cabin about ten and quietly undressed and went to bed, John in the bunk underneath Chen and Ja'in in the opposite bottom bunk. Chen, his head turned to the wall, made no sign that he was awake.

In an hour, when both the men were breathing deeply and evenly, he softly turned back the covers. He was fully dressed. He eased himself softly down to the floor.

But not softly enough. John sat up in bed and yawned elaborately. Chen stepped out of the cabin and turned down to the toilet, instead of the hatch. He heard John fumble on a robe and come padding down the hall behind him.

Chen slammed and locked the bathroom door. Through the small porthole he could see the illuminations of the south shore. The waving trails of light streaked across the bay. He stuck his head out and smelled the cool, salty air. He tried to force out a shoulder. No chance.

John was waiting in the hallway, looking sleepy. Chen returned to his bunk without a word.

Later, staring into the pitch black of the windowless cabin, his thoughts turned to his childhood. Between the ages of six and fourteen, Inman had taken him every year on vacation to the reefs of Halos. They would pick an isolated atoll far from the tourist trails. Inman was an old friend of the fish-herders; there was company when they wanted it. During the days Inman would sit in the shade and play his double flute while Chen went exploring, naked but for his fins and re-breather, carrying a small trident. When the darkness came early to the depths, he would meander slowly home afloat on the powerful waves that swept around the planet unimpeded except for the labyrinth chains of reef and polka-dot isles. Half-asleep, up to his neck in his memories, Chen dreamed he was swimming hard to catch the waves, but big as they were, they would push on by, leaving him to wallow in the trough as they raced toward his home.

About nine in the morning Chen shuffled into the small galley, still groggy from too much sleep. At a small table wedged into the corner, John and Ja'in were sitting over coffee with the cold remains of their break-fast spread before them. The air smelled like fishy bacon.

John gestured to the small stove, sink, and refrigera-tor that filled one wall of the galley. "Help yourself."

There were some undersized eggs in the refrigerator. Chen searched around for a clean pan. Failing to find one, he was trying to rid the dirty one of fishy bacon when Boss came down the steps from the deck. He was dressed respectably in a flared coat and brown baggy pants.

"Ah, Chen. Good to see you. I fear there has been some misunderstanding. Amazingly enough, you ap-pear to be simply what you claim to be. They botched it up again. At least it's over with—too many loose ends, though. Tsk. You can be glad we ran across you. We shall have to get you off the planet without de-lay. . . ."

"Thanks."

"Now, I understand you are a prospector. And the registered owner of a surveyor, number DS-48."

Chen nodded mutely.

"We got your ship for you. No, don't thank me now. It's docked on Kelos." Boss pulled an envelope from his coat. "Here are your papers."

Chen thumbed quickly through the familiar owner-ship papers. But he looked back angrily. They were no longer in his name.

"This is your new identity." Boss handed over a thin plasticine card covered with myriad raised dots. In the center was the embossed name "Rathur, Egel."

"You are a Mandark national, if anyone asks. No one will. Just present this to the city controller and ask for clearance. We will dye your hair before you leave here, and shave off that ridiculous beard. Make a few injections to change the contours of your face—just temporarily. I doubt anyone will recognize you on Kelos. You will, at any rate, leave there immediately if you value your skin. Has your ship been completely outfitted?"

Chen nodded. He pocketed his old papers and new identification. He wondered who had picked out that godawful name.

Four hours later he was sitting in a dark booth at the rear of the Kelos Grand Central Saloon and Smoke Shop, a flaking dingy cave on the third level. The only light came from the front door, open to the cheerless morning streetlights. The barkeep had his eyes glued to the video, leaning back against the bar with a cigarette burning unheeded in his limp hand. Except for Chen, the place was vacant. The tables were littered with the overturned glasses and soggy ashes of the night before.

Chen was smoking a long, thin-stemmed, white clay pipe with the stiffness of an infrequent smoker. He smiled as he surveyed the jumble of close-packed empty tables. He felt buoyant with the first moment of unpursued, unsurveilled peace and quiet he had en-joyed for more than three weeks. Even the lilting hol-low music from the video sounded good. For three weeks he had been pressing against unseen bars. And then unexpectedly they had opened his cell and shown him to the door and said, "Get lost."

Chen remembered Boss's last words with a chuckle. He could step out of that bar now and within an hour be hurtling past the last gravitational tides of this solar system. Boss had left him at the gate of the Kelos shuttleport. They expected him to leave immediately. Well, why not? What was there to hold him here? Who would expect him to stay?

The bartender emerged from behind the bar with a wet cloth and set to wiping off the greasy tables. A soap commercial grated on the video. In an hour the first customers for the day would come shuffling in, bumping against the tables before their eyes became accustomed to the dim interior.

Chen blew a cloud of smoke toward the door and watched it swirl in the light. It was Alsar. That was why he was sitting in this dank bar rather than barreling through space with the throttle wide open. A dull, nagging morbidity underlay his thoughts. He had been bounced around like a billiard ball, and now he was pocketed, out of the game. Or was he? Perhaps it was just his turn to act, finally.

With a prospector's infallible faith in his own hunches, Chen decided to seek her out. He would take the next shuttle down and trust to his dyed hair and false papers. Maybe he would be lucky. He was due for a break.

He rose from the booth. He put his pipe on the bar and turned to go, knocking a chair over on his way out, but not stopping to right it.

"Hey," the bartender shouted after him.

The street was bright and narrow. Chen felt disassociated from his feet. He passed two old hotels, plasticine peeling off the walls and littering the walk. There was a laundry, and a crabbed, hunched-up man stood in the doorway, looking daggers at him through bleary eyes. Chen reached the tube station and hastily punched out the code for the shuttle dock.

The dock had a single ticket window staffed by a middle-aged woman with sharp, squinting eyes and a chin that rolled down her neck. The line was already long when Chen arrived, and by the time he advanced to the window the woman was looking harried and mean. Before he could speak she jumped on him.

"Well, don't stand there gaping, what do you want?"

"A ticket to Arcturus, please."

"Which port?"

He stared blankly for a moment. He didn't want to return directly to Piedsplat, but he didn't know the other ports of entry.

"Damnation," the woman exclaimed loudly. "Make up your mind, balloon-head. You're holding up the line."

"Well, I don't know . . ."

"All right, okay, one ticket to Piedsplat. Sixty even."

Chen dug into his pocket. Then he remembered. How stupid! He was flat broke, or just as well. Boss had given him a credit to buy a cup of coffee. He pulled out his hand empty and grinned ruefully.

"I'm sorry, I don't seem to . . ."

The ticket-taker thrust her head through the window. "I've heard it before. Go on, get out of here, you bleary-eyed jackass! This isn't an amusement park. Go on, stop holding up the line! Cloud cuckoo."

This outburst attracted the attention of a small crowd of people who milled about, waiting to buy tickets or idly consulting the posted schedules. As Chen hastily retreated from the window, he caught a brief glimpse of a familiar face staring at him from the back of the crowd. It was Commander Proun, with a puzzled expression on his face, as if he had Chen's name on the tip of his tongue.

Chen ducked his head and hurried out. He scurried through a dozen divergent passageways before he stopped to catch his breath. There was no hue and cry, but surely it would not be long before Proun fit his face to his name. Perhaps he would not even inform the authorities, but that was a chance Chen could not afford to take. Kelos was too small a city to hide him for long.

The Small Ships Port Authority was a drab gray cubicle wedged in a web of cargo tubes that constantly boomed, thumped, and rattled. The single room was divided by a waist-high neophrene counter. Behind the counter, a small cluttered desk sat in the middle of a large expanse of white linoleum. In front of the counter, eighteen chairs were packed together, turned this way and that. Two front chairs were already occupied. Chen took a chair in the back.

The clerk didn't hurry with the other two men. Chen waited for a tense half-hour before handing over his papers. The clerk punched them into the city's customs computer, and after an interminable five-minute wait, stamped the papers and handed them back.

"Five," he said with a vague wave out the door.

Chen went down a long hall to a small boarding stage marked with the roman numeral five, where a pod had already deposited his ship. He looked at it for a long while. It had been so long.

The forward cabin was a jumbled mess due to the thorough search the surveyor had undergone. Chen hastily stuffed all the loose material into a convenient locker and began checking down all systems preparatory to flight. He barely finished in the ten minutes before the city controller gave him final clearance and popped his ship into space.

He blasted into three fast orbits around the planet, following an erratic course, ducking in and out of the traffic lanes till he was sure he had shaken any tail. Then he set the course which he had predetermined a month before during his sojourn on Earth.

Many light-years beyond Arcturus, toward the dusty heart of the galaxy, he had plotted his run. For the next ten months he would survey it painstakingly in a trajectory that was calculated to section out the space as carefully as a seashell sections out its inner chambers.

Chapter Eight

When his ship had passed the gravitational swells of the sixth and last planet of the Arcturian system, Chen turned the controls over to the autopilot and went back to his cabin to change clothes. He threw the casual suit Boss had given him down the disposal chute, hoping the reclamation unit could make something useful from it after the suit had been reduced to its component molecules. The new liner he had bought on Earth was in the cupboard where he had left it, but the clear plastic wrapping had been ripped open and the liner crumpled and crammed back into place. Chen frowned at this palpable reminder of the sack of his ship by the officers of the *Astrion*, the Arcturian police, and probably Boss's men as well.

He pulled out the liner and flapped it in the air. It hung seamless and unwrinkled, like a silver snakeskin. It was the perfect second skin, both cool and warm, light and strong. He slipped it on, ran his finger down the seam to seal it, and charged it up.

Estimating approximately how long it had been since he blasted off from Kelos, he set the chronometer at four hours even. Then he commenced a thorough examination of the bio-support and mechanical systems of the surveyor. The men who had ransacked his ship had not hesitated to break into sealed compartments, fiddle with every dial, unscrew and unbolt everything that was not welded into place. It took Chen twenty hours of hard, tedious labor before he had assured himself that the ship was well enough regulated that the automatics could take over the fine tuning.

He was rummaging through his tool chest looking for a flexible screwdriver when he came across the strange metal box. It was swept into a corner of the chest in a pile of spare parts and batteries that had been hastily examined and cast aside. But it was no tool Chen had ever seen, and certainly not a spare part of any machine on the ship. He turned it over in his hands suspiciously. It was flat and square and extremely light, just a casing, apparently empty. There were no seams, not even microscopic ones, on the dull burnished metal. Two bearings were mounted in opposing corners. They turned freely and were apparently held in place magnetically, for the box did not enclose them far enough to hold them in. Perhaps it was a bomb, Chen thought. Or a tracer.

Next to Chen's sleeping quarters was a small room of equal size, packed with an elaborate array of instrumentation that functioned as one brain to analyze any rock, liquid, gas, or dust Chen might take an interest in. Wedging himself into the narrow bench seat, he pulled out a drawer and fed the box to the 'spector. In the flat modulated voice reserved for computers, Chen asked for a detailed structural analysis. The machine's response flashed immediately onto a large glass screen in front of him. There was a diagrammatic view of the object along the x, y, and z axes, the trigonometric expression of the curves of the box, and the description: exterior casing, gas-cast carbon; interior, crystallized helium.

"That's ridiculous," Chen muttered to himself. Had someone been fiddling with his 'spector too?

He asked for field readings of the helium. The response was: Mass, none. Spectrum, none. Electro-Magneta-Gravitational Bands: $A = 4.719$, $B = 3.450$, $C = 10^{68}$, $D = 0.000$. . . . Reference, Brigit, *Hypothesis on the Permutations of Internal Stellar Metamorphosis*.

Chen remembered Brigit well. He had had cause to consult his book before. The crystal flower of the *Astrion* and the spike in his pocket, and now this artifact, were all of crystallized helium. And these three were the only specimens known to man—or to Chen, at any rate.

He left the 'spector and went into his cabin. He dialed Brigit's book on the viewer. A better part of it was devoted to a history of the theory of novas—it was all still theory, at that. Chen found the reference he wanted toward the back of the book, where Brigit turned to his own theories about the mechanism of a nova:

> In the instantaneous transformation of the customary chemical and physical processes which stoke the solar furnace, the time-space continuum is strained beyond its capacity. This continuum is, to use a basic mechanical analogy, the drive belt of the hydrogen-helium reaction. Ordinarily, the fission-fusion cycle entails a degree of slack in this belt, and the time warp which is in evidence within the outer limits of the solar corona is a function of this so-called slack.
>
> During a nova, this slack is instantaneously taken up. On the one hand, there is an immense explosion of matter as the core of the sun breaks open like a bombshell. Meanwhile, in the interior of the sun, matter is being driven inward in time and space. In this implosion, matter reaches its crystalline essence, even crystals of helium, hydrogen achieving a peculiar stability. And this essence exists as a unique evolution of matter in this continuum. It is, for lack of a suitably scientific word, a phantom, an avatar of matter. It has form, but no color. You could feel it, but it would have no mass. It would be infinitely purer than a diamond of the first water, infinitely more compact. But its weight, its luster, are held at arm's length in time, in the past or future, it is impossible to say which. These crystals would indeed be the jewels of the universe.

Chen smiled as he ran his eyes over the familiar passage. Stepping back to the 'spector, Chen pulled the artifact out of the feeder tray and replaced it with the crystal spine Inman had given to him. He didn't like the idea of feeding it to the 'spector like any old piece of assay, but he hoped the comparison would be revealing.

The field readings on the spine were not at all what Chen had anticipated. Mass: 2.5473 gm.. Spectrum: none. Electro-magneta-gravitational: $A = 0.00$; $B = 0.00$; $C = 0.00$; $D = 0.00$. In comparison to the helium of the artifact, Chen's memento was dead, energyless. Yet it had mass.

Chen was faced with two facts that were difficult to assimilate into his technical background. First, the crystal of helium in the artifact was *not really there*; it was like the emperor's new clothes, but it had great potential energy. It was removed from this time; it was a reflection in time. Second, someone had obviously worked the helium to put it into this shape, shaped it at the level where matter and energy run into each other. The shell of gas-cast carbon had also been shaped at the molecular level, but this form of atomic architecture was not too far beyond the technology with which Chen was familiar. However, shaping the helium was like working with time itself.

Chen recalled a conversation he had overheard as a teen-ager between Inman and a prematurely grayhaired researcher from Cantelever, a former student of Brigit's. The researcher had been very enthused over the crystal flower which Inman had just brought in. He maintained that the brilliant spectral display of the flower was proof of Brigit's theory, that it was caused not by the diffusion and refraction of light through the atomic lattice of the crystal, but rather by the periodic curve of time displacement of the crystal. . . . The exact theoretical explanation had been more than Chen could swallow, but as Inman had put it to him, it was simply that the light was scattered not through space, but through time.

If that were the case, then this encased block of helium had been stabilized, somehow, at some point in the past or future, which would explain its lack of mass, or any reading on the spectrum. And his crystal fragment would have then been stabilized in the present, its potential energy converted into real mass. Both Chen's keepsake and the artifact were products of the same technology. Chen squeezed his hands at the intuition. So close, but so far. He had discovered a treasure—in his tool chest. He knew what it was, but that was all. Where had it come from? What was it used for? Beyond his flushed imaginings, what did he really know about it? Was it a tool? A fuel cell, a motor? Bomb? Light bulb? Or just a piece of jewelry?

The surveyor, driving at the limit of its power, was finally coming into the sector where Chen had decided to make his run. He began to decelerate and set to work on his detectors, tuning the omni-band eyes of the surveyor so they could accurately pick out the significant warps and woofs in the delicate tissue of space from the background static caused by the dust and gamma radiation of open space.

For a while the mysterious box was put aside as Chen began his run, his ship coasting silently through the ear of space, engines dead. But though he would have customarily been absorbed in his instruments—for it was only by careful attention that the detectors could be fully utilized—this time he found himself absently contemplating the scopes without really seeing them as he returned time and again to the problem that he had wrapped up and put in a drawer.

During meals, he would take it out, lay the box and the piece of clear crystal side-by-side. He would pick them up, turn each over and over, imagining what stories must lie behind the two objects. One day, mentally comparing the box to a gyroscope, Chen carefully outstretched finger and thumb over the bearings and gave it a tentative spin. He had expected it to slip out of his hand, but it didn't. Almost weightless, it spun slowly, picking up speed as he watched, unconsciously holding his breath.

The box grew lighter. The dull sheen of the case blended into a diamond-shaped blur. Then it seemed to throw off bright sparks like an ax held to a spinning grindstone. The room paled. The flashes burst into his head. His consciousness dissolved like mist in the morning sun. . . .

Rolling desperately to his side, he stuck his hands down into the mud of the pool and rose clumsily, yet quickly, slipping on the wet grass, shaking his head to clear the water out of his eyes. A tall man in dark clothes stood over him with knees flexed, a long thick staff drawn back ready to strike again, shouting in excited bursts, "What are you doing here? No one is allowed outside at night! This forest is dangerous. Who gave you permission . . . ?"

The man's tight-fitting helmet reflected the stars from its shiny blue surface. His eyebrows were drawn low over his eyes, his angular face thrust forward. It was the face of the Enemy.

The Enemy was fast. He did not make any effort to go for the gun at his waist as recognition came into his eyes. He thrust the stave forward, aiming for the solar plexus.

The wet, dazed warrior threw up his arm. No one had ever beaten him at free fighting. Even as his mind turned over and over the one thought—"The Enemy, here?"—Luxor acted with the speed of a striking snake. His right arm took the blow hard while his left scooped a handful of water and mud into the eyes of his enemy. A lightning kick caught the tall man with the stave before he could aim his gun, and another kick broke his neck before he hit the ground.

Luxor's right arm was numb to the shoulder, broken no doubt. He dragged the body off into the bushes. Wrenching the dead man's helmet loose, he studied the still face carefully. There could be no doubt. The Andere too had escaped the nova, and come back to haunt them.

Returning to the pool, he looked down at his own helmet resting on the rocks at the bottom where he had dropped it. He was trying to hook it out with the staff when a noise sent him flying back into the wood. He took the blue helmet and the gun as proof.

Stopping in a small glade not far distant, he glanced

*up at the sky to fix his directions. Behind him, he could
hear distant shouts muffled by the giant ferns. His
breath came in a ragged rhythm. The nova lay straight
ahead. It would guide him back to the settlement. Hugging his crippled arm to his side, he was running, running. . . .*

Luxor stared for a full minute with wonder at the
spinning box in his hand. It slowly slowed and stopped.
No, wait, he was not Luxor, he was Chen. Chen. His
consciousness rose slowly like a bubble wobbling up
through oil; it burst; he found himself once again. The
experience he had just lived settled into his memory.

"Holy hell." Chen dropped the box on the table with
a clatter and tried to spring to his feet, but didn't quite
make it. His memory raced wildly over the experience
once more, searching for some clue to help him understand it. He was afraid it would fade and vanish
quickly like a dream upon waking, but it did not. Every detail remained crystal-cut and clear; he could still
feel a vague tingling in his right forearm where he had
blocked the stave. The memory refused to assimilate itself into his subconsciousness; it floated like oil on the
water.

Chen looked at the quiescent box with awe. Now he
had some idea—however vague—of what it was for:
memory recorder, transmitter, or maybe book, movie.
But he did not think the vivid images could be dis-
missed as imagination or fiction. The icy numbness that
throbbed between his elbow and his wrist, the dull ache
in his lungs, the clarity of recall all screamed, "It's
real!" The experience kept running around and around
in his head, like a film flapping at the end of the reel.

The nova. There was a marker he could fix upon,
even if it were at the opposite end of the galaxy. Unless
. . . Unless all this had not even happened yet. Unless it
lay in the far-distant future. And with this question
came another. Luxor—that seemed to be his name—
was he human? He felt human. Chen had slipped into
his skin without a ripple of revulsion, of foreignness.

And the anxiety, the anger, the surge of fear and re-pugnance—those had all been human emotions. Even the Enemy—Chen could only think of him in those terms—had looked human. He had crumpled when struck, had died as Chen himself would have died. And yet . . .

The sky. That was what had been overwhelmingly alien. It was so luminous, not like a night sky at all, a sky so bright that the expanding cloud of the nova had appeared as a gray blotch, a spot of grease on the fab-ric of the heavens. And in the welter of thoughts, in the fleeing panic, Chen could clearly distinguish the thought, Selenor-home-family-nova-death. So this had been Luxor's home star.

Chen started searching the star maps. It took him a long week with the astrogator to find the nova. It was an arduous process, and a machine could have done it better and faster. But Chen had to rely on his memory, hoping he could recognize that bewildering jumble of stars once the astrogator has postulated their position for him on the mock-up screen. Starting with the most recent nova and working back, he checked every nova that had occurred within thirty light-years of galaxy center. He had to view each one from at least a dozen positions, for he could not possibly recognize it from any position that did not approximate Luxor's vantage point. Within his working radius there were maybe three or four novas that occurred every year. After the first dozen, he began to feel a slight headache, which quickly grew to migraine proportions. He finally stopped for the day, for fear that he would forget what the original pattern of stars had looked like.

In order to refresh his memory, Chen tried to start the box once again. It refused to work. Exhausted and without food, he fell asleep in his chair twenty hours after he had innocently picked up the light metal box and gone spinning into someone else's mind.

When at length he located the nova, he recognized it almost immediately. It took a while to bring it into the correct focus, but so indelibly had Luxor's mind imprinted its image in Chen's memory, there could be no doubt. The thick mass of stars that would have bewildered most people was as clearly marked as a street sign to Chen. The nova had exploded more than a century ago, some twelve or thirteen light-years from galaxy center. It lay along the same spiral arm of the galaxy that held the Empire of Man. Once Chen had sighted in the stars as he remembered them from the night sky of Luxor's fern planet, it was an easy task to locate the colonist's star.

Luxor's second home star had also gone nova, sixty-eight years ago. Chen's right hand twitched. Unconscious of his own instinctive fear, he wondered what curse was pursuing these people? Surely that was no coincidence. The worst misfortune in the universe could not be that implacable.

By the next day Chen was convinced that it was more than plain bad luck, much more. He had decided to take a look at the two novas through the ship's optics, which, though not as large or precise as a moon-based observatory, nevertheless had a superb range in the interstellar vacuum. The two dead stars lay close together in the sky, so Chen could get them both on the scope at once. Chen was looking practically straight on along an imaginary line laid between the two novas, extending out along a major arm of the galaxy. However, the original nova was partially obscured by the brilliant expanding cloud of yet another burst star which lay even closer to Chen, at a distance of less than twenty lights. The third nova was even more recent, too—thirty-two years old.

Chen dropped back into his seat and switched off the scope, as if the menace he felt was suddenly staring at him through these three distant eyes.

He saw it all too clearly. The dark sockets of the Enemy, the intent angular face, staff raised to strike. And then the blow, the crazed ravenous sun bursting inside their heads.

Across the void, through a century, this ghost had come hunting him. As it had come hunting Inman too?

Those three novas were the milestones of a path that led straight out this arm of the galaxy, and Chen—and the Empire of Man—squarely straddled the route.

With the barest hesitation, he set a course for the nearest nova. That dead shell was beyond his cruising range, but he wasn't going there. Somewhere along the way he felt sure he would stumble across what he was looking for.

Chapter Nine

Passing close by the last inhabited star on the frontier, a G5 with two terraformed planets boasting a combined population of over five million, Chen drove out into the Standish Rift, a great empty passageway that cut into that arm of the galaxy. Though the rift lay close by a major population center of the Empire of Man, it had never been well surveyed. Across that gap, even the nearest stars were far away, and these stars were either planetless or too cold or too hot to support a colony without prohibitively expensive terraforming. Even if there had been planets suitable for colonization on the other side of the rift, the distance would have been too great to sustain the trade upon which every fledgling colony depends for its existence. Consequently, this frontier had long since been abandoned in favor of more accessible routes of expansion toward the center of the galaxy.

Chen's surveyor was driving at a little better than ten lights. This was the best any small ship could hope to attain, for the velocity of a ship cruising beyond the speed of light is dependent on its mass as well as the power of its thrust. For this reason, large ships such as the *Astrion,* which plied the breadth of the Dominions, could attain cruising speeds far in excess of Chen's maximum capability. The surveyor was built compact, light, and strong, with an eye for atmospheric maneuvering as well as deep-space cruising. And though the small ship's mass was negligible in comparison with the *Astrion's,* his powerful engines could equal a quarter of her cruising speed.

The speed of light had once been believed to be the highest velocity attainable in ordinary space. The "Einstein heresy" had been refuted early in the days of interplanetary exploration. However, the speed of light had proved to be the "inertial ultimate." Any speed beyond that of light must be maintained by constant acceleration, and if the thrust is cut, the ship quickly drops back to the velocity of light.

Chen slipped quickly back into his old routines. There was much to do on the first days of the run, and he quickly forgot about everything but the immediate demands of prospecting. And luck was with him. Three weeks into the rift, he found a moderately good cloud of molybdenum dust. He could have staked a claim and headed back, but he decided to pass it by. The find didn't thrill him as it should have. It wasn't satisfying. He did not bother to set up a beacon. Chen drove on, stopping less frequently now to check his instruments, but checking them with more care.

At the end of a month he was well into the rift, probably farther than any man had ever penetrated. He was nearing the end of a day's run when he hit a dust cloud.

At the speed of light it would not have been much of an obstacle. The dust was about one molecule—mostly hydrogen and helium—per cubic yard thick. At ten lights it was like running into a storm of locusts in a crop duster. The hull shrieked and shivered, and Chen was up and diving for the controls even before the alarm came on. The drive automatically cut out before Chen could stop it manually. The pressure-sensitive doors slammed into place, locking him in the control room until the danger was past.

It was over in an instant. Picking himself up off the floor, Chen lurched over to the light board and checked down the systems. The hull was badly scored in places, and one L-tube was leaking radiation, though not yet at a dangerous level. Only the ship's aerodynamic streamlining had saved it from more extensive damage. Nevertheless, it was serious enough. Chen damped the L-tube and balanced the thrust before the surveyor began to oscillate. Now, unless he hit anything more substantial, he would make it eventually to the nearest star system, cruising at two lights, his top speed with one tube out. He would be lucky to salvage his life. The little ship would never be the same.

When he had satisfied himself that there was no damage that he had overlooked, Chen turned his attention to the detectors. The cloud, spread out now on the rear screen, was strange both in composition and form. Instead of the spherical mass that gas naturally forms as it slowly coalesces over the aeons, this cloud was a fine, dense sheet, stretching out past the limit of Chen's detectors. The cloud was almost entirely composed of hydrogen and helium atoms, being devoid of any of the heavier elements which usually can be found in small quantities in these gas clouds. The lack of heavier elements, and its tenuous form, made the cloud hard to detect from a distance. The density of the sheet would have made it fatal to any larger, faster ship than Chen's.

Turning his attention to the forward screens, Chen found something more ominous and unexpected than the presence of this bizarre cloud. Close by was a large spherical body, a planet floating alone, unaccompanied by sun or moon in the depths of the rift. Chen was relieved to see it, for it would probably furnish him with the requisite materials for repairing the ship. But he was uneasy, for in all his years of wandering between the stars, he had never encountered a planet so isolated, so out of place. He had found slag, icebergs, gigantic asteroids holed like Swiss cheese, grains of salt as big as an interstellar cruiser. But this planet was a little bigger than Earth. And that cloud was fast taking on all the ominous significance of a trap in Chen's mind.

Chen braked sharply and swung toward the planet, cutting his engines as he approached, swimming silently into the gravity of a planet which he still could not see on the optics. He went into an elliptical orbit, shaving close by the surface at a dizzying speed, swinging high out over the other side of the airless planet. In the dim starlight he could not see much detail. He set up the relay cameras and regularized his orbit, running around the planet till he had photographed it all in one long pass, like you peel an apple, from top to bottom in one unbroken strip.

The sensitive photographs and other instruments told him much. The planet was covered with a fine linen cloth of powdery snow and sharp ice. Underneath, protruding in splotches that glittered in their own dark fashion, was a thick coat of hard glassy slag, frozen into puddles five, six hundred miles across, and miles deep. Everywhere the glassy obsidianlike rock reflected the chalky snow, sending the starlight rebounding in crazy rills, showing tessellated fields of silver and crystal, black diamond mountains with razor edges, and tideless oceans of powdery frost in whose depths the ice flowed like water. In places the heat of the interior of the planet broke through the constraint of this solid cap of hard rock, sending great clouds of steam shooting miles into the air, turning instantly into huge snowflakes that plummeted down through the airless cold to add their weight to the immense snowdunes.

Desolate as it was, it was a prospector's dream, as Chen was quick to realize. There was no topsoil to dig through to get to the ore-bearing rock. Great chunks of rich ore, already bonded together, could be blasted loose and towed away through space. It was a find unequaled in the history of prospecting. Under the conditions of the Armansport Homestead Act, no prospector could make a claim on any habitable planet. This normally restricted them to the scraps of heaven, the refuse of space. But under no conditions could this planet be considered habitable. It did not matter if it was far from the tradeways. This planet would create its own tradeway.

It was also, as Chen turned his mind to more pressing matters, quite suitable for his repairs. He had only to pick a flat pan of rock free from too thick a cover of snow and set down. The landing would be facilitated by the lack of atmosphere, which ordinarily would have inflicted more punishment yet on his punctured surveyor. It was almost too convenient, he thought. Too still, too untouched.

Instead of landing immediately, he spent another full day in orbit, watching carefully for any sign of activity, any irregularity. But the planet offered him no explanation, no sign. It was unresisting when he dropped small explosive charges in three locations to get an accurate seismic reading on the structure of the crust. He found it was fused solid right down to the molten sea of minerals which supported it.

Still, one small yet significant fact kept him on edge, kept him up for forty solid hours watching the screens in indecision. The fragment of crystal helium which Inman had given to him—this lucid piece of crystal, previously as clear as well water, was now throbbing with myriad colors!

With his suspicions unallayed, Chen set the ship down on a barren table of rock after a fitful night of rest and a light breakfast. The blast of his jets sent a shower of snow cascading in all directions. He carefully checked his detectors before making any preparations for debarking, but there was still no sign of life. He set the alarms.

Chen got out the equipment he would need and looked it over once more to see if it had been tampered with by the investigators. He selected two long slender glassine canisters and mounted them on a back frame, coupling their short tubes into a larger hose that ended in a trigger-nozzle. He suited up then, and dressed down with the speed and precision of an experienced prospector. He got a broad fine-toothed rake with a telescopic handle from the locker and clipped it on his belt. Once he had verified his communications and control link with the ship, he picked up the back frame and stepped into the airlock.

With the two canisters pressed against his belly, it was a tight fit. The light above the hatch glowed green, and he hopped down onto the slick, hard surface. The door rolled closed behind him, shutting off the light. Chen swung the pack onto his back, switched on his chest light, and started off in a slow shuffling gait, fearful of slipping on the hard glassy surface.

In order to patch and bond the hull, he needed varying quantities of five different metals. The L-tube was a separate problem, requiring not only the ordinary patching and bonding, but also a more complicated inner liner.

In the two canisters were a solvent and a catalyst. Chen walked a good distance from the ship. Luckily, there was no wind to worry about. He found a slight depression in the rock where the solvent wouldn't spread. Setting the trigger for a radius of three feet, he directed a fine stream of mist at the ground in front of him. The solvent and catalyst blended as they came out of the nozzle. The thin covering of snow cleared, and the rock underneath became beaded, as if with sweat. The rock seemed to lose its cohesion, and a puddle of liquid quickly formed, perfectly circular and six feet across. The puddle was a dull gray color, but had a strange translucence. Chen waited till the surface of the pool was calm. Now the liquid was mirrorlike, quicksilver.

He "primed" the pool with a fistful of nuggets of pure copper. Unclipping the rake from his belt, he set the teeth for a distance of four millimeters. He pushed a stud at the base of the handle, and the rake expanded to a length of ten feet. Being careful not to get his boots splattered by the solvent, Chen raked out the pool. It was about two feet deep. The smooth bottom yielded a large enough pile of small copper nuggets to satisfy Chen's needs. He had to rake quickly, for already the surface of the pool was clouding, as a thin layer of metal salts formed. In a half-hour the puddle would turn into a shallow bowl of coarse, tarnished salts. He waited till the solvent clinging to the copper had turned into salt, then picked the nuggets up, and brushing them off, dropped them into a net bag woven of fiber glass. The canisters rode lighter on his back, their contents sloshing back and forth as he started back to the ship, following his footprints.

Imagine Robinson Crusoe's dreadful surprise when he came across the bare footprints of a native on the shore of his island refuge. So when Chen first saw the prints of boots almost identical to his own coming around the surveyor from the other side, merging with his own footprints, leading right to the airlock, he thought of Crusoe leaning over those tracks in the sand, his hands clutched tightly on his flintlock. Crusoe melted into the jungle, but there was no foliage here, just a hard pan of rock dusted with snow. Chen stopped in front of the airlock, his mind dead calm, deliberate.

He walked around to the other side of the ship. The footprints led off to a distance of fifty yards and stopped short. The intruder must have come from the air. Chen searched the sky, but he could not discern anything against the black velvet background. There could have been an armada a half-mile up, and he would not have had an inkling.

Walking purposefully back toward his surveyor, Chen adjusted his nozzle to a needle spray. The airlock popped open. Stepping inside, he tensed his muscles. The space suit hung loosely on him as the small chamber pressurized. The green light flashed on, and the airlock opened inside. Holding the nozzle forward, Chen stepped in.

A figure in a tight-cut black space suit was sitting at Chen's chart table with his back to the airlock. As Chen entered, the man swiveled calmly around to face him, clicking down the dark visor on his helmet as he did so. His right glove was off, and in his hand—a human hand, well manicured, with small curling black hairs on the back of the fingers and above the knuckles—was the enigmatic metal box which had occupied Chen's attention for so long. Chen didn't speak. His nozzle was trained on the intruder's chest.

"Where did you get this?" the man asked, his voice coming small and tinny through the throat mike.

"I'll give you thirty seconds to get off my ship." Chen's finger tightened unconsciously on the trigger, and a thin mist curled up from the nozzle, filling the small cabin with a smell like that of battery acid.

"It is you who are trespassing," the intruder said, even softer than before. "This is a serious matter. You are lucky to still be alive. However, you could help us out, perhaps. . . ." Chen's uninvited guest put the box in a pocket of his suit. "We would like to know where you got this box. We will reward you very handsomely for the information. You must tell us all you know about it."

Chen didn't respond. He was trying to analyze the situation before it got out of his control. He couldn't very well dissolve his visitor into a puddle before he had found what he was up against. The solvent would wreak as much damage on the ship as it would on the man. Chen sidled over to the detector bank and activated the scanners. A single glance confirmed his fears. Close overhead, a huge ship waited, posed like a cat ready to pounce on a canary.

"Can you speak to your ship?" Chen asked.

"They are listening."

"Well, tell them you're a dead man if they don't let me lift off this planet."

"I'm sorry, but I don't have the authority to do that. It's really out of the question. If I were not expendable,

I would not be here. It is merely a question of whether you come along freely, or do we have to coerce you?"

"Who *are* you?"

The man stood up. He was taller than Chen, careful and ponderous in his movements. "Surely you must realize the seriousness of this situation," he went on, ignoring Chen's question. "As a prospector, you can appreciate what an incredibly lucrative find this planet is. My employer is not at liberty to reveal his identity at the moment. There are delicacies of the law. The find might be contested." His tone was conciliatory now. "Of course, we *must* know how you happened upon this planet."

Chen suddenly placed the man. There was no cartel behind this, he was sure. The man was really interested in the box and nothing else. He was a policeman, a soldier perhaps. He wasn't bargaining with Chen, he was forcing him into a corner. Chen considered bluffing. He didn't have any alternative, actually. He couldn't flee with a busted L-tube advertising his presence like a neon sign to any ship within two lights.

"All right. I guess you do have a right to know how I got here. It was just an accident, really. I didn't mean to barge in on anyone's claim."

"What about the box?"

"Oh, that. Just a souvenir. I picked it up on Melinda. It contains crystallized helium, you know. Don't know if it's much good for anything."

"I'm sure my employer will be glad to hear about it." The intruder gestured to the airlock. "All right. Let's go. You first."

The ship that came down to pick them up did not look like any spaceworthy vessel Chen had ever seen. Like the space suit his interrogator wore, it was without markings. It was a perfect globe, but it was not the shape that was strange, it was the surface. The ship was not just bright, like polished metal; it was mirrored. It seemed to reflect the stars with more intensity than they burned with through the airless sky.

From a distance, the mirror surface gave the illusion of smallness. When they approached it, it loomed so high above them it seemed about to roll over on them. Chen was used to the whales that ply the ways between the stars, but those ships were always built piecemeal in space and flown from orbit to orbit, far from the full gravity of a planetary surface.

They walked toward the ship, not seeming to get any closer. Far above them, a small square appeared in the waist, and an open skimmer floated out, gliding down to meet them. They mounted the plain circular disk. The pilot, without so much as a glance in their direction, twisted the grip of the simple joystick that rose from the middle of the disk, and they smoothly ascended into the hatch.

The interior of the ship was as simple and overbearing as the outer shell. They emerged from a gigantesque airlock onto a vast unfathomed expanse of black velvet. Aside from a distant pinpoint of light, Chen's eyes could discern nothing beyond the myopic lights of their skimmer. It was impossible to gauge the size of the chamber; it swallowed up the hiss of their passage without the slightest reverberation as they slid toward the point of light.

The single light came from a spotlight planted high on a wall over a large door. It cast a small circle of light over a haphazard array of skimmers. They landed directly in front of the door. Two men in space suits awaited them. Chen was led down a long barren corridor, lit only occasionally by unhooded lights.

His aerometer told him the air was safe to breathe. Chen cracked his faceplate. A nervous sweat was threatening to overwhelm his suit's reduction capability and mist up the inside of his visor. He welcomed the breath of air against his face. The atmosphere was almost tropical, seventy-five degrees Fahrenheit, and very humid. Overlying the familiar smells of steel, oil, and plastic there was a musty vegetable scent in the air, like raked-over moldy leaves. The dark yielding floor swallowed sound as well as light, so the noise of their passage was muted and deadened.

They walked for more than a mile before they came to a steel bulkhead which blocked the corridor. A very ordinary light bulb hung on a cord above thick pressure-sensitive curtains. They entered a lower, broader hallway paved with flagstone and decorated with murals of a lush, tropical jungle surmounted by a blue-green ceiling. The flagstones were worn down in the middle of the corridor, as only centuries of use could wear them, but the murals were as bright and vibrant as if they were still not quite dry. The corridor was long and had few exits. They passed several portals where Chen remarked the seared and jagged slashes left where the doors had been forcibly removed. They met no one.

They came to a second curtain, not a pressure curtain designed to close off an area from any sudden drop in atmospheric pressure, but a rich brocade curtain with a golden sheen. Chen passed through the curtain first, followed only by the man who had brought him here from his surveyor.

Inside was a large domed room, oval in shape and dominated by a large circular table on a raised dais. The massive table was surrounded by more than twenty high-backed chairs. Eight of the chairs were already filled with men in the anonymous black space suits that reduced them all to ciphers. The room contained a dozen armed men, idle, but intent. Every faceless faceplate turned on Chen as he entered. The man who had captured him turned to the table. He gestured toward Chen. He was making an explanation to the men at the table, but Chen could not hear it. Chen shifted uneasily on his feet as he looked around the room.

The tall man turned to him. "Take off your suit."

"No," Chen said, more to gauge the effect of his refusal than with the intention of offering any real resistance.

He was seized from behind by two men. He jerked

loose and staggered a couple steps forward. "All right, all right." He unsealed his suit slowly, folded it neatly, and laid it in a pile at his feet. The tall man bent and picked up Chen's suit. He turned it inside out and examined it minutely.

Chen was about to speak, just to break the heavy silence, when a wailing siren jerked the room into action. The man who had captured Chen dropped the space suit and ran to the big table, where he took a seat with the others. Chen approached the table. It seemed to be the control board of the ship. There were many lights, and at each seat, a checkerboard of buttons. "Get him the hell out of here," someone shouted, a hint of fear in his voice.

A shudder seemed to pass across the floor. All but a few of the armed guards rushed out in a jumble. Before Chen was hustled out of the room, the ceiling dimmed and became an open view of the space around them, and he could see, here, there, and again, the little red traces of other ships. Were they under attack?

Two men muscled him out another door and down a narrow corridor. Each holding an arm, they forced him to a trot. As they rushed down the corridor, Chen felt the gravity go spongy under his feet. The three of them crashed into one wall, and then the other. The ship was maneuvering desperately, straining the intragravity beyond its capacity. Chen cursed himself for a fool. Why had he come along so docilely?

They came to a rough wooden door which had been incongruously wedged into the frame of a metal archway which was ripped and torn. One of the guards opened a padlock. They pushed Chen inside and slammed the door behind him.

Chen found himself in a large storage room. A jumble of wooden crates and boxes had been swept in disarray into one corner of the room by the shifting gravity. When those boxes start tumbling again, Chen remarked to himself, it's going to be touch and go. Overhead, one light on the end of a long dangling cord swung wildly to and fro.

A violent lurch sent him skidding down into the corner where the crates were stacked ceiling-high. The room reeled. The wooden crates groaned and shifted. Chen tried to crawl up the smooth, steep floor away from them.

Another vigorous shift of the gravity whipped the light bulb up against the ceiling. It burst with a dull pop that seemed insignificant, even comical against the background of shrieks and belly-rumbling tremors that wrenched the ship. The stack of crates came apart with a noise like a felled tree, catching Chen up in a short, mad avalanche to the other corner of the room. He went out like the light.

It might have been a few seconds or hours later, Chen awoke and wiped the blood from his eyes. He was pinned against the cold wall of the corridor by a burst wooden crate. The makeshift wooden door of the chamber had burst under the pressure of the rampant cargo and was hanging in shards from its frame. The ship was still moaning and bucking. Chen managed to free himself from the debris and roll out of the way just as another surge of seesawing gravity sent a new wave of splintered crates rolling out into the corridor to break against the wall opposite the door.

He pulled himself to his feet. Nothing seemed to be broken, but from the sound of the ship, he wondered if the whole monstrous structure was not about to come apart.

If the ship was going to break up, Chen wanted a suit. He took off down the corridor in the opposite direction from the control room, slamming against the walls, sometimes falling down the length of the floor, sometimes pressing himself flat to keep from rolling back the way he had come.

The corridor ahead was lost in darkness. The light behind threw his shadow far forward, growing dimmer as he plunged on. He finally left the square of fading light altogether behind him and groped along with one hand outstretched, the other tracing along the wall to his right.

A jar brought him to his knees. He put his hands out to ward off the floor and fell forward. His hands plunged into empty space; the floor had come to an end. Two more steps in the dark and he would have walked right off into a pit. The rough torn edge of the flooring dug into his chest, ripping through the tough material of the liner. Slowly he levered himself back into a sitting position and backed off on his hands and knees from the pit. High above him the ship was whining in a pitch almost out of hearing, and he felt now, rather than heard, the thrum of the drive.

The intragravity was holding steady now, and the background noises slowly dimmed their frightening oscillation. He felt his way gingerly up to the edge of the pit again. Lying down, he felt out into the darkness as far as he could reach. Nothing. He shouted to see how close the acoustics were. The echo of his voice came back muted and distant. He rose to his knees and felt higher. A round metal bar waist-high barred the corridor. Holding onto this, he felt out the dimensions of the walls. They were glass-smooth up to the lip of the cavity, where they had been shattered and twisted, leaving sharp, clutching shards.

Chen had already decided against turning back. But to go any farther, he must see. He rose and felt out a sharp razor-edged spike of metal. He purposely and very cautiously used this to rip open the sleeve of his liner. From the tear he pulled a long kinky wire which his fingers recognized by its spring stiffness and the small bumps spaced an inch apart along the wire. This was one of the heating elements of the liner. By shorting it on the powerpack in his armpit he could obtain brief yet intense flashes of light, each flash consuming another inch of the filament.

The first flash revealed what Chen had already seen with his fingers—the end of the corridor, a torn, warped flange of burned, bluish metal. Beyond it was black. Chen leaned out over the bar and shorted another section of wire. In the harsh, unyielding light of the brief flare he could make out the great dimensions of a ragged hole torn in the tissue of the ship, its crumpled edges disclosing the honeycombed lattice of adjacent apartments.

The charred remains of chairs, desks, tables, draperies, and carpets could be seen shifted into the corners, leaving nothing distinguishable, nothing to give a clue to the origin and nature of this chaos. It was a hellhole, a black maw with sharp teeth of metal that glittered in the darts of light. The air was filled with the dry, gagging dust of decay.

Chen was about to turn back in despair when he noticed the rope dangling from a stud of metal at the edge of the passageway. He thought perhaps he could use it to descend, but when he pulled it up in the dark, it proved to be less than ten feet long. It was a new rope, slick in his hands, with knots to grip. Chen decided it could only be used to gain the adjoining chamber, hidden behind the outcrop of steel wall to his right. He pulled against the rope and found it strong enough to support his weight.

Giving himself a good deal of slack, Chen swung out off the bar past the saw teeth of the wall. He came easily to the other side of the wall, landing in a cloud of dust, doubled over a row of moldering padded chairs. The short flashes of his liner's heating filament revealed what had apparently once been a large auditorium. Several rows of dusty chairs faced a stage which was no longer there, blown away with the first few rows of chairs, knocking the next rows back into the laps of those chairs yet farther back. Chen clambered over the debris, holding his breath as the padding came apart under his feet and hands, filling the air with a powder so fine it would be long before it settled. Every ten feet he would stop and light another flare. The sleeve of his liner hung in tatters up the elbow as he unraveled the filament bit by bit. He used three flashes to investigate some bones in the rubble. They were human, as far as he could tell.

He passed out of the auditorium through a large door which opened to the touch. Beyond was a room

that was worlds removed from the ruins. His eyes
blinked and watered in a bright, warm light. A soft
clean carpet of dark red stretched across a spacious,
low-ceilinged room. All along three walls, green plants
grew in profusion, falling from their trays to creep along
the floor, their long blue-green leaves half-curled, like
the fingers of a strong hand at rest. The air was filled
with the pungent smell of the tiny blossoms. Chen approached the plants in amazement. But as he stretched
his hand forward to touch, the vines curled back up
into their trays. Along the one wall where the plants
did not grow was a low pallet, a chair, and a chest. A
few books were scattered beside the bed. Chen went
over to investigate.

"Stop!" The voice came from a few feet behind him.
"Don't turn. Hold your arms out in front of you."

Probing fingers passed rapidly over his body, feeling
for a weapon.

"Turn around."

Chen turned slowly. She was retreating slowly, her
gun held steady. Recognition struck them both at once.
She dropped the gun. He dropped his hands, and they
stood for a moment there, amazed, like two dumb cows
on the verge of a ditch.

———◆———

Chapter Ten

Alsar reached out and touched him lightly on the
arm. Her hand was cold and taut.

"Chen," she said. "Then it was you, in that ship?"

He picked up the gun and tucked it in his pocket.

"But how did you ever find us?"

"I didn't find anyone. I was down for repairs on that planet. I might ask you the same question. Whose ship is this, anyway? If you thought I didn't know what was going on before, my ignorance then was nothing compared with what it is now."

"I'll explain, but we can't talk here. They might come looking for me. Christ, you look a mess. Did they beat you?" She opened a narrow metal door. It was dark beyond.

"No, a crate fell on me."

After many turns and a few long stairways, they came to a small, neglected room. Alsar propped her small flashlight against a counter and turned her attention to Chen. This room looked like it had once been a bedroom. Beside a round dirty bed there was a chest of drawers, a sink, a counter, and three chairs. Chen tried the faucet. It didn't even gurgle. Alsar tore off a piece of the bedding, shook off the dust, and tried to wipe clean the worst of Chen's cuts, wetting the cloth from the water bottle of her own space suit.

"This is the Ship-That-Gives-Life. It was a gift from Manhome to a people that are now dead, wiped out in a war of attrition that spanned half the breadth of the galaxy. The ship now belongs to Darlan."

"Darlan? Manhome? What has Earth got to do with this? Ouch! Gently."

"Sorry. The Earth knows nothing of this ship. Only Darlan and his crew, and now you. It is the closest-guarded military secret in the history of the Dominions."

Chen hesitated. His head was buzzing. Deep in the guts of the ship, the silence was thick and palpable. "Then Earth is not the home of man?"

"No."

"But these are men, aren't they?"

"Yes. Arcturians." There was a bitter tinge to her voice. "I told you. The people on this ship died. Long ago." She rose. "All right. Come with me now. You're not seriously hurt."

"Where are we going?"

"To a place that's safe."

"That's what you said the last time."

"Wasn't it safe?"

"I don't know. I didn't stay. Alsar, whose side are you on, anyway?"

"And you? I might ask you the same question."

Chen pulled out the pistol and pointed it at her. "Alsar, I am in a desperate position. Don't play games with me. I don't want to use this. I have never killed a man—or a woman—but if it is necessary to get out of this alive, I will not hesitate. I am not about to risk my life again because of a stupid sentimental attachment to you."

Alsar stood up, then sat down. She shrugged her shoulders. "I will explain it to you briefly. I am the pilot of this ship, ostensibly under Darlan's orders. The ship has just been in a battle, as you know, and it is severely damaged. I am probably the only person who can cope with the damage. If you don't let me go, none of us will live through another day. I was on my way back to the control room when I came across you in my quarters."

"You're going straight back to Darlan and tell him where I am," Chen accused. "You're Darlan's pilot. Why shouldn't you turn me in to him?"

"I am not Darlan's pilot! I am the pilot of the Ship-That-Gives-Life! I will never abandon this ship as long as she flies. Since you do not have confidence in me, and I don't have time to argue with you, I'll leave you to your own devices. . . ."

Before Chen could stop her, she had knocked the flashlight to the floor behind the counter and darted out the door into the dark corridor. He pointed the gun but did not pull the trigger. He retrieved the light as her steps faded into the distance. Knowing the way, she could run faster in the dark than he could follow with the light. Already she was lost to him in the maze of deserted chambers and passageways.

This time he decided to wait. He shut off the light and stretched out on the floor. The ship had ceased her labored groaning, but Alsar's last comment about the ship being in danger kept sounding in his ears. If the ship was going to bust up, he wouldn't have a chance. There were few inner airlocks, and the pressure curtains would give you only enough time to get on your suit—if you had one.

Chen set out from the small room, not quite knowing where he was going or what he was looking for, beyond the desire to get a suit. At least, now he had a light.

Eventually he came to a lighted corridor where signs of frequent traffic made him fear a confrontation with Darlan's men. He had emerged from a dark corridor through a thick pressure curtain on which a small placard had been pinned: "RESTRICTED AREA." He stood for a moment blinking in the bright fluorescent light, undecided whether or not to expose himself in this part of the ship where he was vulnerable to the first chance passerby. However, he was not likely to find an empty suit in the deserted part of the ship.

He had not advanced far down the bright corridor before the sound of conversation came to his ears. He turned and ran softly back to the entrance to the restricted area. The conversation faded; apparently the men had taken a turn. Chen was discouraged.

He parted the curtain to take refuge again. He would lie here in ambush, he decided. That was a better plan. The thick darkness was congealed into an even darker shape which blocked his path. The smooth obsidian shield of a helmet visor reflected the lights of the corridor. Before Chen could drop the curtain and run from this terrifying apparition, taking advantage of his lack of a suit, the figure caught him by the wrist.

"Lost?" the thin voice inquired. Chen recognized the accent of the man who had lured him into this ship.

Chen's mind clouded with rage. At every turn he was frustrated. How long had this silent figure been dogging his footsteps? Chen seemed to cleave down the middle, and as one-half of him watched dispassionately, the other half reached for that brittle globe of reflecting black, and with a scream of rage and pain, Chen caved it in with his bare fists.

A cry of pain broke from the suit, not tinny and static, but agonizing and afraid. Chen's body crashed into the slick and puffy suit. The man gave a step but did not fall. Chen felt his own hands caught up in the vise-like grip of the power-assisted gloves. They stood for a moment immobile, neither giving, locked in an isometric death struggle. Through the shattered visor ringed with brittle shards, the face of his antagonist was glazed with a red sheet of blood welling from the cuts on his forehead and cheeks, the eyes maddened, reflecting a bull anger, mouth parted, the lower lip hanging slack.

As the feeling left his hands, Chen stumbled back under an irresistible force until he felt the cold steel wall at his back. The intent face, as hard as granite, bored into his soul, and a gasp of recognition was wrung from him.

"Darlan," he sighed.

A spark of recollection, of recognition kindled a colder light in the eyes of steel. The power-assist gloves suddenly released their grip on Chen's hands. They fell to the beaten prospector's side, drained of blood and feeling. Chen tried to massage one deadened hand with another, equally numb and slippery.

"Why don't I kill you?" Darlan asked, almost teasing. "Do you know why I don't?" Darlan's hands were shaking with repressed anger despite the heavy steel-mesh gloves.

A stampede of men swept around them as a dozen soldiers ran to Darlan's rescue. They caught up Chen and wired his hands together behind his back. The pain left them as they went numb once more. Darlan stood still as a medic dabbed at his cuts with an antiseptic pencil and a wad of plastiflesh. An oily stream of sweat mixed with blood ran down the Herald's cheeks.

The soldiers cut off the remains of Chen's liner piece by piece to make sure he had no weapons. Chen didn't take his eyes off Darlan, nor did Darlan cease to regard him with a cold, malicious stare.

Chen's gaze was distracted by an exclamation from one of the soldiers who was furrowing in the pockets of his shredded liner. The soldier held Chen's little spine of crystal up to the light. It glowed like a trapped rainbow. Chen was too beaten to feel despair. There went the last shred of his alibi of ignorance—ignorance of the memory box, the planet, and Darlan's ship. But what did it matter? He was as good as dead now.

Darlan followed Chen's gaze to the fragment. The Herald pushed aside his medic. "Give me that," the Herald said, and took the gem from his soldier. Darlan bounced it in his hand to test the weight, then held the crystal up to the light. Every man was mesmerized by the scintillating fires that seemed to leap, like lightning, from the tiny spine. When Darlan looked again at Chen, it was with an entirely different expression, of perplexity, puzzlement, and a suspicion of fear.

Darlan walked off, turning at the last moment to call, "Dress him and bring him along." Four of the soldiers and the medic ran after the Herald as he walked briskly down the shiny corridor, the crystal clutched in a tight fist.

With Darlan gone, the others gathered around Chen to stare. There was a hint of awe in their voices as they murmured conjectures, predictions, suspicions. They could not understand the current of events any more than Chen himself. What had their commander been doing chasing after this man alone in the dark confines of the restricted zone? Few of them ever ventured into the unlit bowels of this ship. The live faces of the dead rose up, it was said, and came hurtling out of the dark, holding you stillbound and paralyzed with fear, unable to raise your weapon or your voice.

Even Darlan himself seldom visited the dead quarters. The Herald's first act, after leading them on board some months ago, had been to post conspicuous warning signs all around this portion of the ship. Only the woman, their pilot, was suspected of walking these defunct passageways. She often disappeared for long periods of time during ship's-night. Some said she had a lover, and that they made their trysts in the dusty beds. Who the lover could be was the subject of much idle speculation. Many possibilities had been raised and quickly debunked. The two most popular contenders for general approbation were: one, a ghost, and two, Darlan.

Thus Chen's appearance under such mysterious circumstances had raised a surge of curiosity and anxiety that rattled the ship's personnel quite as much as the surprise attack by a fleet of Dominion cruisers. Darlan's crew was the cream of the Arcturian Space Fleet. They took orders from Darlan alone. But they found themselves treating Chen with a sort of diffidence that they themselves were hard pressed to explain. Though not a one would admit it, more than one felt the chill of superstitions he had never realized he possessed. The strangeness of this man, found alone on a dead planet, who disappeared from his prison into the bowels of the ship, only to reappear hours later locked in combat with their Herald, stirred their fears to such a pitch that they felt every familiar corner of this ship become as alien and threatening as the first day they had come aboard, fearful of coming face-to-face with an alien around every bend.

They led Chen back to the control room. The same tense men were still at their posts around the command table. They had their helmets off now, and they looked no more friendly without them. Alsar was absent.

There was a long moment of total silence.

"Will you loosen these bindings?" Chen asked. No one moved. He repeated the question, louder.

"Give me some clothes," he said. He was shivering, stark naked in the airy, high-ceilinged chamber. He turned to catch a guard staring at him dumbly, his mouth parted and his brow creased in puzzlement. Chen addressed his request to the man again. The guard turned his gaze to the men at the table.

Darlan came up behind him. "Take off those thongs and give him some clothes." The men jumped to obey, startled because they had not seen the Herald come in, so intent had they been on the naked figure of Chen.

Darlan's face had been washed clean of the last vestiges of their struggle, and only the ridges of plastiflesh showed where he had been cut, a light brown against the pallor of his face. In the eyes which calmly studied Chen there was no trace of rage. He was in control. He reeked of assurance.

Darlan turned to the men that manned the command table. "Leave us." In seconds the room was empty except for the two of them.

"You are not what I thought," Darlan said. "Why did you go to Balder-wa? Where did you get the box and the sunstone?"

Chen did not answer. He was slipping into a dark liner, like the one that Darlan himself wore.

"You may be surprised, but I have reason to be grateful to you. So far, I've taken all this on a bluff— the ship, Arcturus, soon the Dominions. I've taken it all on a bluff. But now, it will cease to be a game."

But Chen was lost in his own thoughts. Sunstone, Darlan had called it. That had been Inman's word, too. Could it be coincidence?

"Do you think I will use it?" Darlan asked.

"What?"

"The sunstone. Are you going to pretend you don't know what it is for? *We* don't have to play games. When I saw your ship down on Balder-wa, I thought, this is some devil of a prospector who has stumbled on it, just as I did years ago. But now I am not sure at all. You do not look like an Andere. But where else could you have come from? Why have you come back like this? Answer me!" Darlan screamed.

"I'm just a prospector."

"What were you carrying around a sunstone for? Did you steal it? Where? Did you find it on this ship? No, because I've already turned the ship upside-down. You don't know how hard I've looked. And now you come out of nowhere and drop it right into my lap. That's too much. You are Andere, or they have sent you.

"Perhaps you were going to sell it to me? Perhaps you would like to see me use it? You will see." The anger was rising again in Darlan's eyes. He walked up to Chen and unexpectedly slapped him hard across the face. "I always said you would make a murderer out of me, too. And you did."

Darlan walked over to the command table and thumbed a button. "Stations," he said. "Bring me the cartel negotiants and the Dominion prisoner."

A crowd of men bolted in the door and quickly filled the room. They all noticed the white mark of Darlan's hand on Chen's cheek.

The Herald stood mute and implacable till his crew had taken their seats. "Set a course for Anasthenon," he said. Chen knew the name. It was a G-2 he had passed on his way out into the rift, an unpromising star with three inhospitable planets and a Dominion Ranger station.

"Where the hell is Alsar?" Darlan asked. "Page her." He turned to Chen. "You sit down over there. Behave yourself, and I'll keep you alive a bit longer."

Chen took a seat on a low bench that ran along the same wall as the large door. He hoped that when Alsar came in she would not notice him, dressed as he was in one of Darlan's own uniforms. And she did not when she ran in a short time later.

"Where were you?" Darlan demanded.

"Taking a walk," she answered tersely.

"We are setting a course for Anasthenon. How extensive is the damage?"

"It will take a year to repair without the facilities of a major shipyard. But we can make headway. Darlan?"

"What?" he said sharply. He did not like to be questioned.

"Who was it that attacked us?"

"The Dominions. Who did you think it was, Atilla the Hun? They've been hunting me for months, ever since they suspected the existence of this ship."

"Are you sure? You must be sure. I agreed to help

you teach your men to fly this ship, but I am not going to pilot her into another battle. Is that understood?"

"It is inevitable, Alsar. It was the Dominions. I have proof. There is no turning back now."

Alsar sank dejectedly into her seat. "They should never have attacked us. They should have known. What will happen now?"

"Don't worry, we've proven we can handle anything that they throw at us. There were twenty-three of them, and not one ship got away." There was no mistaking the satisfaction in Darlan's voice.

"Oh, no," she said. Then, for the first time, she noticed Chen. She paled.

"We took only one prisoner. As evidence," Darlan continued.

"Evidence? Evidence for what? This is war. When those ships don't return, no one will need to guess who's responsible. So you stood off twenty-three. Now four hundred will come hunting you, and you will die, Darlan. You will all die!" she shouted to the room.

Darlan stepped close to her till his face filled her vision. "No, my little pilot, they won't, and we won't. And do you wonder why?" He pointed to Chen. "Do you wonder where he came from? I will tell you. He is an Andere!"

"No!" Chen jumped up. "Alsar, I am not the Enemy."

"Then how did you know 'Andere' means 'Enemy'?" Darlan asked. The Herald looked to Alsar and nodded, and Alsar looked at Chen with a new light in her eyes, with loathing, fear, and hatred on her face.

Then Chen realized. It was the language of Luxor, who had met the Enemy in the fern forest of a world removed in time and space. *"Andere, ya m'po Andere,"* and then the blow, the pain, the kill, and the flight. "No," Chen said. "I saw it in the box. It was Luxor, the warrior."

"Darlan, don't try to scare me with your talk of Andere," Alsar rebuked him. "He had one of those boxes, that's all."

"No, that's not all," Darlan said. "There's something else, something more concrete that will convince you."

"What?"

"You shall see shortly," he teased her. "I won't trouble to go into it now." He turned toward the door as a contingent of men came in. Chen was startled to recognize the faces of the five stolid men he had seen last in the library of En'varid's lodge on the *Astrion*.

They were followed shortly by three soldiers who dragged in a tall, bedraggled man dressed in the uniform of the Dominion Navy. His gaunt face turned slowly this way and that, striving to absorb, record everything, looking already for revenge.

"Commander Nurbury," Darlan introduced him to the room at large. "Of the Dominion Navy, isn't it?"

Nurbury looked over, and his jaw dropped. "Darlan," he said.

Turning to the cartel negotiants, Darlan said, "You saw how we were attacked without warning by a fleet of the Dominion Navy. Is this not what you too can expect from the Dominions? Will they not ride upon you with the same arrogance? This one"—he pointed to Nurbury—"we will send back to Earth with a note from us. You, gentlemen, I will send back to your organizations with what I am sure will prove to be a most convincing demonstration of the military superiority of Arcturus."

Darlan turned to the command table. "Can we get Anasthenon on the optical yet?"

For an answer the lights went out and the dome of the big room dissolved into a vertiginous panorama of outer space which came down to the floor level. Chen got up off the bench, where he appeared to be leaning out over a sheer drop into space, so perfect was the illusion. Near the top of the dome, a yellow star waxed bright. They were closing on it rapidly, and Chen marveled at the speed that had already brought them so close to a star which he had passed a month before he came across the planet of ice and slag. Already Chen could make out the crescents of the three uninhabited planets.

"We are getting a call signal from the Ranger station."

"Ignore them," Darlan instructed. "Bring up in the shade of the prime planet.

"Gentlemen," the Herald said, turning to the cartel negotiants, "you are about to see a weapon which will indisputably prove the folly of resisting me. You will need no other persuasion, I am sure." A dark smile played briefly across his face. "Nor will the Dominions, when they get the report of Commander Nurbury. Not that they will need an eyewitness. The whole galaxy will be our witness."

The sun waxed huge in the dome. The giant ship pulled up behind the shadow of the prime planet, a dark velvet mass where shadows were piled on each other. It overreached half of the curving view screen like a huge maw already sucking them in.

Darlan turned to a large taciturn man who had up till then sat silent and unoccupied at the command table with his hands folded across his chest.

The man straightened up.

"Launch the weapon," Darlan said, and no one in the room missed the softly spoken words.

The man pressed a button. He pressed another. Then he settled down in his chair.

"All right," Darlan said. "Full acceleration away from the sun. Keep in the penumbra of this planet. Make it fast."

The others on the control board went to work, but Alsar remained dead calm. "What weapon?" she asked

"Just a small demonstration. It will be safer to view the results from a distance. About one light should do."

"One light!"

"We don't want to miss the scope of it," Darlan said.

The bright sun was already receding rapidly, dwindling first to a small golden dot, and then just another silver spot in a sky where much brighter stars held the attention. They all waited in silence, some wondering, some bored. Only Chen felt sick. He turned his head away. He didn't have the heart to look at what was coming, what he knew was coming, and he didn't have the guts to scream.

"There is . . ." Darlan started to say. A cascade of light flooded the chamber, leaving no shadow in the large room. A dazzling, madly groping octopus of light surged out of the ink-black night. They all hid their eyes in their hands.

"Every sun is a potential bomb!" Darlan shouted. "And I have the fuse!" Darlan seemed to bask in the fierce light which had driven others to their knees. "That is your proof, Alsar. He brought it. I tell you, he is an Andere!"

Suddenly the great blinding light was extinguished. They seemed to rise on the crest of a wave. The gravity buckled underneath them, knocking them all over like tenpins. A fury of lights was winking on the control board. Alsar, wedged into her chair, was playing her fingers desperately over the keys of the board with a celerity born of fear and long practice.

The view screen came back on. The stars and distant galaxies were pinwheeling, spinning rapidly around them. The effect was dizzying and sickening. "Turn it off," someone shouted. But even as the men huddled in pockets where the disaster had thrown them, the stars slowed and steadied. The nova was at their back, and not on the view screen, but its aurora climbed up the walls from the floor, obscuring the heavens. Arcturus, far ahead, lay at high noon.

One of the cartel negotiants approached Darlan. "Herald," he said softly, "I am sure you will not use that on any inhabited systems. You would not do that."

"The hell I won't. I will destroy any star that opposes me. And there won't be any Resettlement, either. You don't resettle a cloud of gas. What planet do you come from?"

The negotiant paled in the pale starlight. He allowed himself to be pushed aside by another negotiant. "Herald," the other said, "let us make no pretensions of altruism. I am sure you are fated to become a new moving force in the history of the civilized galaxy. My cartel will deal with you on any terms you dictate. We ask only a few trade routes here and there to be allocated to us alone, a few way stations."

"I ask nothing less than your total and unquestioning obedience. Six leaders cannot win a war. One can do it. You will get what I give you, when I decide to give it to you. Or else I shall gut you all."

Darlan's assurance, that of a poker player who has just drawn four aces, dominated them all. He ground on the faces of the negotiants with his gaze for a minute. Then he turned to the command table, to the seat of his pilot.

"Turn back to Arcturus," he said.

The seat was empty. Alsar was gone.

Chapter Eleven

Darlan turned to his soldiers. "Find her! Search the restricted area, search every part of this ship. Bring her back even if you have to hurt her. And be careful. She's dangerous."

As Darlan turned to the command table again, taking a seat at the circular console, Chen took the occasion to absent himself from the room also, following on the heels of the search party. He attracted no attention in his black liner. All eyes were on Darlan, and Darlan was occupied.

Chen kept the retreating backs of the search party on the edge of sight. He had no trouble keeping up with them, but he shortly encountered two men coming toward him down the corridor. He was tempted to duck down a divergent hall he had just passed, but the men had seen him, and it would look suspicious to double back. He advanced on them, keeping his eyes straight ahead. They didn't look twice at him.

Chen breathed a sigh of relief. Surely Darlan would soon notice that he too was gone and send out the alarm. An idea stopped him in his tracks. He spun around and went noiselessly gliding down the corridor after the two Arcturians. Before them, at a short distance, lay the small divergent hallway which Chen had forsaken. Chen paced silently a few feet behind the men, gauging the distance. When they came level with the side corridor, Chen sprang on the outside soldier, grabbing his pistol as he fell, jostling the other man into the hall. The gun was unfamiliar. Chen pointed it at the other man, who was armed and still on his feet, and pulled the trigger. Nothing happened. The other soldier, finally realizing he was being attacked—in his own ship by a man in his own uniform—drew his pistol. Chen found the safety on his weapon and released it, and fired again. This time it took effect. Though there was no sound, the soldier slumped against the wall.

The man's disarmed companion froze, half-risen from the floor, as Chen turned the pistol on him. Chen motioned him into the side corridor and followed, dragging the other guard by his limp arm. He saw now what had caused the man to fall. Three small darts were lodged in the chest of his suit. Chen picked them out and put them in his pocket.

"Take off your suit. Fast."

The other soldier hastened to comply.

"Your liner too," Chen said. He was afraid his own might be bugged. The soldier stood shivering in the cool draft of the empty corridor.

"Lie face-down on the floor with your hands outstretched. Do it!" Chen started changing. "What's down this hallway?" he asked.

"A kitchen and a mess hall."

What should he do? He could meet guards coming from any direction. "Do you know the way to the restricted zone?"

"Yes."

Chen sealed up his seams and slipped on the helmet. It was a good fit. "All right. Get up. I want you to run there, a short distance ahead of me, at a pace I can follow. If you break off the path, I'll shoot you down." He prodded him with the pistol. "Go, damnit."

The soldier took off in a rabbit trot down the well-lit hall. Chen found himself hard-put to keep up with the man.

"Slow down," he shouted. The man speeded up. There was a door just ahead, and the man was going to turn in. "Stop," Chen yelled as loud as he could. "Stop right there or I'll shoot!"

Just at that moment three men armed with rifles emerged from the door. The naked man screamed at them, waving his arms madly in the air. Chen raised the pistol and sighted on the soldier's back.

A blinding flash split the air. When Chen could see again, the body of the soldier was on the floor. Another burst of lightning from the rifle of a Guard made it twitch. The three guards ran up to the body, and Chen did too, not daring to flee now, forced to bluff it through. No one paid any attention to him.

They were clustered around the body. More men came running. Half of the face was burned away, the other side caked with blood.

"I guess that must be him. . . ."

"But I thought he had dark hair. I saw him."

"Perhaps. Well, call up Darlan."

Chen edged his way back down the corridor. A little way off, not even out of sight of the men, was a door marked with the red sign that meant refuge to Chen. He slipped inside. The air was still. Turning up the amplification of his suit, he could hear little pings of dead silence. He ran off as fast as he could, following the round light of his chest torch.

Darlan's voice came over the communicator, advising his men to look out for Chen. Then the Herald addressed a few words to Chen himself, telling him what a fool he had been, that he would lose himself in there and come out begging for water in two days—and then they would kill him. Chen switched the communicator off.

Well into the maze that led on without end, Chen took a moment to sit down on the floor of a moldering apartment. The bed, he was sure, would have collapsed into dust under his weight. Now that he was safe for the moment, that survival mechanism which preserves one from paralyzing fear in moments of extreme danger ran down, and Chen broke into a cold sweat; tremors shook his frame.

After a short rest, he went on in the dark, following the small bright circle of light cast by his chest light on the dusty floor, sometimes metal, sometimes stone or wood. He was soon hopelessly lost, as Darlan had predicted, and Chen himself had expected.

He found himself in a section of what had apparently been offices. There were broad desks and narrow chairs, strange machines of woven strands of wire, curled like hair and studded with jewels, encased in a clear hard covering that was coated with dust. There was a soft, firm carpet on the floor. Chen decided to stop here. Why go on? He was sufficiently lost.

He cracked the plate of his helmet open and took a grateful lungful of fresh air. The floor felt like a feather bed. In two minutes he was in a deep and dreamless sleep.

He awoke with the silence pulsing in his ears, as if just shaken by a sound. There was another—the distant murmur of voices. Angry voices. He could not make out the words. He rose to his knees in the impenetrable dark. Should he flee down the corridor away from the voices? Instead, he found himself going toward the sounds. He turned up the amplification in his suit. Now he could make out the words, but the tongue was alien, though Chen had heard those lilting accents before—in

Luxor's memory. Their speech had an irregular cadence and the range and clarity of a bird's song. The long, drawn-out humming of the last syllable of each sentence blended with the reply, producing a constantly shifting harmony, sometimes pleasant, sometimes jarring.

Soon Chen saw a light. He advanced faster. The soft luminescence was coming from a large room with a few chairs gathered around a single large table. The corners of the room were lost in shadow. A dozen people in loose robes grouped around the table on a floor of polished stone inlaid with copper.

Chen watched from the impenetrable darkness of the corridor, just beyond the threshold of the room. Across the room, the other entrance gaped as black.

The voices churned up the silence. The shadows waved as the people gestured, turned, replied, accused. The light, from some unseen source, seemed to concentrate in the center of the group, giving the outer members a slight halo. Chen could see two men in the midst of the group pushing each other, screaming, and yet always addressing the crowd, pointing out the other, denouncing.

The shorter of the two men danced back and forth in the steady light. His silhouette showed the dent of a poorly healed busted nose; his lips were drawn tight. He shouted, "Damn you! You can't get away with that!" He raised his hand, threatening, and his antagonist—who had only been waiting for this—struck out as fast as a snake, staggering the smaller man with a spearing blow to the solar plexus so he flew through the tight ring of onlookers, stumbling back and falling on his shoulder.

The tall, heavy attacker was grabbed by three of the assembled crowd, but he shook them off with a ferocity they were not prepared for and attacked the shorter man again, landing a kick on the side of his neck with all the force he could muster. A dull thud cut off the shorter man's efforts to rise from the floor, and he collapsed, unconscious, in a heap. Purposefully, the tall man knelt astraddle his victim, and wrapping his hands around his throat, squeezed till the veins stood out like blood worms in his forearms. The ten witnesses strained to pull him from the defenseless man, but he kicked and bit and elbowed, and nothing could pry his fingers from the man's throat.

Chen advanced a step into the room. Was he going to let this happen? He fingered the dart gun. No one had noticed him. He stepped back into the shadows, undecided. The man on the floor had spoken English in the heat of the argument. Who were they? Humans or aliens?

Slapping down the visor of his helmet, he ran out into the room. No one looked up as he raced across the short distance which separated him from the two struggling figures. He shouted, and his amplified voice cut into the hysterical cries of the aliens. He brought up short and reached out to grab the shoulders of the tall, implacable strangler.

He grasped empty space. His hand went right through the man's body.

Chen swore to himself, and none of the actors paid the least attention. "It's a trap!"

Still, there was no sign of the trapper. Chen turned to steal back into the night, when he was stopped dead by a word.

A new character had made her entrance from the unseen off-stage. Running into the midst of the group was a woman more beautiful than daylight, and she was screaming, "Inman! Inman!" in a voice of desperation.

Except for the man stretched lifeless on the floor, everyone turned to the woman. The tall assailant got up, and as he slowly unwrapped his fingers from the throat of his victim, the other men rushed forward to draw him off the limp body. A look of defiance came over the victor, but the woman did not give him a second glance. She bent over the man on the floor, holding him, crying, covering his face with nervous caresses, trying to coax a spark of life from him.

The assassin stood over the woman and addressed

her a bitter reproach. She raised her musical voice to overbear his own, and in long guttural words that broke like shell bursts, heaped scorn on him, and cried and shook her head in frustration and anger. The blood drained from the tall man's face, and he made one terse statement that hissed out under pressure between his tightly clenched jaws. He pushed roughly through the tight knot of men and disappeared.

The woman did not watch him go. Long sobs like waves washed over her body, and every time she murmured the word "Inman," Chen felt a hand of ice shake him by the spine. He could have reached out and touched the delicate backbone of the anguished woman as she knelt. Others helped her to her feet and led her away. Four men grasped the limp body of Inman, and as they lifted it, Chen could clearly see the lolling head and had no doubt that it was indeed his foster father—a young Inman, his face still unmasked by the lines of worry and tragic memories which Chen had learned to trace there.

Chen felt tears roll down his cheeks. Was this not a nightmare, peopled with his own imaginings? All the characters seemed to have that deep-set familiarity that even strangers take on in your dreams.

The light faded; the people thickened into darkness and slipped away, leaving Chen standing alone in the middle of the room, his chest light on the floor, where the layer of dust had lain undisturbed and untrampled for many years.

The overhead light flickered on. Alsar stood in the opposite doorway, half-submerged in shadow. She was fully suited, but Chen recognized her by the outline of her breasts in the tight tunic. He stepped toward her.

"Stay where you are," she said sharply.

Chen opened the visor of his helmet. "But, Alsar, it's me."

"I knew that. Anyone else would have run, except for Darlan. I no longer trust you. It was no coincidence that brought you to this ship. If you are not of the Andere, what led you into the Great Rift to Balder-wa,

the dead planet of these dead people? How you had me
hoodwinked! Just as I was keeping an eye on En'varid
for Darlan, so you have been keeping an eye on me.
And now you have brought your dirty spawn back to
Darlan—I mean that solar bomb. Do you think you
can control him? Do you even care?

"Darlan has broken and betrayed one race, and now
you'll see another racked up on his wheel of hatred.
Why do you drive him on?" There was acid hate in her
words. She was baiting him, and Chen was afraid of
her.

"Alsar." He stepped forward. Suddenly she had disappeared from the doorway, only her hand protruded
into the light, a dart gun aimed at him.

Chen backed up. "I have never been more or less
than what I seemed to be," he said. "I have always
drifted. I don't have much of an identity. Never saw
my real father. Live by scavenging. You have to trust
me. I came to help you."

"Go fawn over Darlan. He likes that."

"Darlan wants to kill me."

"I believe it, but what makes you so sure?"

Chen told her about the naked crewman that was
gunned down by mistake.

"That doesn't make you my ally. You gave him the
fuse for that bomb, didn't you? Was that your idea of a
joke? Do you think I like being a fugitive in my own
ship? Yes, I will give you back to Darlan to torture and
kill. You can tell him for me that I'll destroy this ship
before I let him use her for war."

"Let me explain, Alsar. Please. I was raised by a
prospector. When he died, he gave me a bit of crystal,
like that of the flower on the *Astrion.* He never told me
where he got it, or what it was for. I only knew that he
had found it out beyond Arcturus, and that there had
been a great tragedy, for he came back a broken man.
Darlan took that piece of crystal from me. I don't
know, but I think he used it to cause that sun to go
nova. I had no idea!"

"I don't believe you. There was only one Earthman

that came here among these people, and that was Darlan."

"But that broadcast, those people. You ran it, didn't you, to lure me in here?"

"Yes."

"Don't you know who they were, the two men fighting? And the woman?"

"The tall man who won the fight, that was Darlan. That was my father."

After a long silence, Chen forced out the words, "And the other man?"

"I don't know. Darlan never explained it to me. It's from his personal horde of mnenocasts, and I'm not supposed to have access to it. I've been using them to scare the crewmen out of here. The woman—I don't know who she is either. I don't understand the language."

"That man is Inman, the man who raised me. He gave me the crystal. He was here, and he fought with Darlan."

"So you say. I have no reason to believe you. I grew up on this ship, after the Andere came and gutted it. Darlan and I were the only survivors. I was too young to remember the fight, but I know much about this ship. She was my mother. But of my people, Darlan will tell me nothing."

"If Inman were still alive, he would be about the same age as Darlan, I guess. They must have come across this ship together. It could not have been coincidence. But what were they fighting about?" Chen's mind floated back over his memories of Inman, seeking a clue. Why had he never mentioned Darlan to Chen?

"Alsar, will you trust me?"

"How can I trust you? You are a talented liar."

"Play it over. Perhaps we will see, understand."

She considered for a moment. She dropped the pistol and stepped out into the room. "All right. Come with me."

Chen preceded her under a watchful eye into a small adjacent room. A large plate-glass window separated the two rooms. Alsar went to a desk and yanked open the top drawer. There was a clatter of light metal as she rummaged through it. She selected what she wanted and slammed the drawer shut. On top of the desk was a flat metal box the size of a shoebox. She lifted the lid to load it.

"Wait," Chen cried.

She spun on him suspiciously. "What is it? Don't startle me like that. These darts are lethal."

"I'm sorry. That tape, box, whatever. I have seen one like it. It is the same as the one I found in the cabin of my surveyor."

Alsar nodded. "I wondered what had happened to that. En'varid had it. In the rush, I was careless."

"But don't you know?" Chen exclaimed. "You don't put the thing into that shoebox—you hold the box in your hand, and you will enter into the scene. It will transpire like a dream, in your head! I did it with the box. That's why I know what the Andere are. I was Luxor, last of the warrior caste from a fern planet. There are murals of the planet on this ship."

"I know nothing of this."

"Try it. Try it, and you'll see!"

"What happens?"

"You enter into the scene, become one of the characters."

"But this is a cartridge for a solidocast," she insisted. "Will I lose consciousness?"

"Well, yes. This sounds crazy, I know, but . . ."

"Then you try it. I don't trust you, though I am beginning to doubt that you are really Andere. You're crazy." She handed the box to Chen.

"Will it start from the beginning?" he asked.

"It always does."

"I'll sit down."

"Help yourself," she said coldly.

Chen fit the box into his hand and gave it a spin. He did not look at it this time. He looked at Alsar, standing over him with her gun. He did not look, but the flashes crept into his eyes, flooding his sight.

"What's the matter?" he heard her ask, and then she was buried beneath the sea in a drowned world as he kicked, struck out free, bursting up to the surface, where open air and light flowed freely. . . .

This was the first anniversary of their discovery, and the two of them were celebrating it with a mixture of elation and homesickness. Already the last outpost of Earthmen lay long since forgotten in a far field of stars. All around lay the great deserted gap which separated their home arm of the galaxy from the next of the twelve great arms. In the speeding vessel, more a home than a ship, they were in the midst of friends and companions, but the vast distance that cut them off from their own species left them with a gnawing unease. They were used to being off along the frontier, but this distance was more than that, much more.

Darlan swirled the last bitter dregs of his home brew in the broad bottom of his wooden cup. They were surrounded by a whole, healthy race whose culture, language, and prejudices were at war, deep within them, with their memories, their morality. It was a war which he and his partner were losing, Darlan reflected. Every day, it got a little worse, as even the most intimate, the most unnoticed prejudices came to light.

Throwing the yeasty dregs of his drink on the floor, Darlan brimmed up his cup again, and refilled that of his partner. This was the first drink they had had together for months, and they both secretly hoped that a little alcohol would dissolve the growing disenchantment and distrust that had grown up between them. They had prospected together for two years and had developed an ability to tolerate each other's weaknesses. Now, for the first time, living in a culture that seemed to offer no food for the yeast of hatred, they found themselves reacting to each other like two male baboons disputing their role in the hierarchy.

The last to go of all the prejudices were the sexual ones. Darlan recognized his own problem. Even though Inman was more jovial, more openly at ease with the people, Darlan knew it bothered his partner too. Both of them had come from distant origins in the intractable soil of new colonies, where self-discipline was survival, and discipline was not limited to a ten-hour work day. "Grubbing puritans," the spacemen would later call their parents. But every spacer had been raised in the dirt, and that was something they would not forget.

They were surrounded by women, sincere and anxious to make love with them. No strings attached. There was no sexual possessiveness, no jealousy. "Don't you see?" Inman had said to him. "They're sane. We're crazy. How can you be jealous? How can you possess an act?"

But that was exactly what Darlan wanted to do. He wanted more than just acceptance in this society in which they were apparently condemned to live out their lives. He wanted to possess a piece of it, a woman to call his own. For Darlan, it was not enough to fall in love with the whole culture. He wanted to fall in love with a woman.

And he had. So had Inman. Out of more than seven thousand women, they had both fallen in love with the same one. Diastre. The others were beautiful, maybe even more beautiful. But they were also unearthly, and their alienness made the two Earthmen feel uneasy. Diastre looked so familiar, so pleasing. She had quickly preempted all their sexual fantasies, and soon they were both to be seen accompanying her, happy at first to be sharing her as two men who share the rising light of dawn and think what a nice day it promises to be. They played mad games with her. Inman charmed her with his double flute, and Darlan with his rollicking stories of rampages of half a hundred planets.

But that had ended, months ago, all the sport. Ended in jealousy and a hatred which they were ashamed to show to anyone but each other, their own private little hate.

Darlan drained his fifth cup and stood up, a bit dizzy.

"Sit down. Where're you going?" Inman turned from

his alien friends to ask. "Have another drink. Good
beer! Best beer within fifty lights!"

Darlan scowled and pushed away the proffered bottle. "I don't want any more." *He sounded sullen and
morose to himself.*

"Drink up, damn your mouth. We can't have a celebration without getting drunk. To our anniversary as
outcasts!"

*Darlan knocked the bottle on the floor and turned to
go.*

"Darlan, wait!" *Inman cried.* "Where do you think
you're going?"

"None of your damned business where I'm going.
I'm going where I don't have to listen to your threadbare stories. . . ."

"You're going off to find Diastre, aren't you?"

"Shut up!" *Darlan screamed.* "What of it? Isn't it my
turn yet? Where were you last night? I looked all over
this ship and couldn't find a trace of either of you."
*Now that he was started, he couldn't stop. There was
so much pent up inside of him. He felt the eyes of their
alien friends upon him, but he went on.* "You don't
deserve her. You lie about me behind my back. I'm
warning you, Inman, if I catch you with her again . . ."

"You'll what? What?"

"I'll kill you." *He spat out the words.* "You run after
her like a dog. It's disgusting. She doesn't love you. She
pities you. She loves me. She wants me!"

"I've tried to make you understand, you bull-headed
bastard. She loves us both. Can't you understand?
What do you want from her? You want to own her?
She's just a piece of ass to you. You're rotten, Darlan.
You'll never see. But I'm not going to let you poison
her with your hate." *Inman waved his fist under Darlan's nose.* "Damn you. I won't let you get away with
it."

*Darlan lunged over the table. Inman was borne
down to the floor; Darlan's eyes burned into him, burning even after Inman had gone limp. . . .*

When Chen awoke, Darlan was leaning close over

him, watching for a sign of life. When he saw that Chen had come to, the Herald stood up and backed off a step. Behind him, Chen could see Alsar hunched over, leaning against the wall with her legs drawn up under her. When she saw Chen sit up, she said, "It was awful, the expression on your face. . . ." She had a large red welt on the side of her face where Darlan had slapped her.

"So you're Inman's son," Darlan said. "He was more clever than I imagined. He got away."

"He just raised me. I'm not his son."

"Who told you that?"

"Inman did." Chen rose unsteadily to his feet. He could feel the acid clinkers of Darlan's extinguished hatred in his own body.

The Herald approached Chen and placed his hands on the young man's shoulders. "This explains much about you that I just couldn't understand. I want to cease this animosity. I might be your friend. All you know is Inman's story. Inman's memories. What harsh things he must have said about me. Tell me!"

"He didn't talk about it."

"Well, I will tell you the truth. The truth. And perhaps you will learn not to hate me so much. I know Inman must have poisoned your mind against me."

"You're a murderer, Darlan. And you made a murderer out of Alsar as well. I don't need Inman to tell me that."

Darlan went on compulsively, ignoring Chen's remark. "We came on the Lelos entirely by accident. We were deep into the Great Rift when we came on Balder-wa. We ran into that screen of dust just like you did. It's the remains of an immense defensive screen they had thrown up around the planet. The Lelos had returned to see this planet, for it had once been their home. They alone had survived the nova which destroyed it, and then, after it had cooled off, they had come back to see if any traces remained of their ancient homesteads.

"There were no traces," Darlan went on, holding

Chen hypnotized. "But they found us there, patching our ship. At first they thought we were Lelos, and then they suspected we might be Andere. They took us with them, for they were hunted, and the far-reaching vengeance of the Andere was still haunting their tracks. There was nowhere they could settle in peace and be sure the Andere would not happen by and ravage their sun.

"They were on their way out of this arm of the galaxy, down the Great Rift and into the Great Gap. They didn't force us to accompany them—'enchanted' would be more like it. They were beautiful, intelligent, and unique in their social harmony. But they were also timid and small-minded. Only the oldest of them had seen the open sky or played in the fields when he was a boy.

"They liked us, of course. After months in space and a shipwreck, we were delighted to rest with our rescuers. Dallying, as Inman would say. Any woman was ours for the asking, and I don't think there was one I didn't ask for. Since no one had any children by either me or Inman, we assumed that our species weren't able to cross-breed.

"And there were food, games, music—so much to amuse, not to mention the ship, which is a miracle in itself. No one person understood it completely. It was a gift from a far older and unimaginably rich civilization, the *real* home of man, it was said. It was a furtive gift to a race of fugitives. Their last defense against the Andere was also their best—flight.

"The Lelos did everything to make us feel at home among them, for we were their *de facto* captives. They were too humane to kill us and too afraid to let us go, for fear that word would get back to the Andere somehow that there were Lelos still alive. We didn't regret it, at first. We were bound for the other arm of the galaxy; we had the run of the ship and not a bit of work to do: adventure, amusement, education.

"But we got on each other's nerves even before we got jealous over Diastre. You know how she looked, but you can't realize how she came to represent everything we had lost, every sweet and unbound breath of air from a hundred planets, every homesick desire compacted as day after day we irrevocably lost any hope of returning. Only Diastre could relieve us, let us laugh. We didn't speak to each other of it, but the thought was on both of our minds: with our surveyor, which we had remodeled and fitted with one of the Lelos' engines, one of us could make it back. But it would never hold enough food, air, and water for both of us.

"Then, one day, shortly before a year had passed, we learned that Diastre was pregnant by one of us. We didn't know who. It mattered little to Diastre whom the child belonged to. She was going to be a mother soon, and that made her happy. But Inman grew more and more remorseful, and as Diastre chatted gaily between us, we would trade silent looks of hatred over her lovely body.

"You know what happened. You saw it as I saw it, and I don't envy you the privilege. Something broke in me, and I nearly strangled him to death—thought I had, in fact. And then Diastre came upon us like that. She ignored me. I could see it was Inman she had loved all along! That bitch. They all looked at me with such a strange look on their faces. Alien, so alien it made my skin crawl. I ran off. They would have killed me. I fled to the hold where our ship had been stored. I started her up in the hold and blasted my way out with the forejets.

"And I swore, if it was the last thing I'd ever do, I would get even with that bastard Inman."

Darlan had been talking rapidly, his account coming out like steam bursting from a pressure cooker, so long had it been bottled up inside him. He stopped and wiped his palms down his thighs. He looked hard at Chen to dare him to disapprove, to beg him to understand. Behind him, Alsar had turned her face to the wall.

"And I did have my revenge," Darlan continued. "It

took me three years. Years of hardship, near-starvation, and the incredible boredom of waiting, always waiting.

"I went back to Balder-wa. I went back with a small atomic bomb, and I set it off. Some facets of the Lelos' technology had led me to believe that perhaps this would alert the Andere of my presence. I had to wait on that bleak rock for almost a year, but they did come. They were as hard as obsidian. Five or six of them could pry your mind open like a can of sardines. That's what they did. It was horrifying. They opened me up, and they saw my hate, my revenge, and their quarry. They were as excited as hounds on a scent.

"So they took me with them, in a cell. They fed me once a day and never talked to me. I was glad of that. They frightened me. I didn't mind the wait. It wasn't as long as I had anticipated.

"One day they came for me. They wanted my help. They had sighted the ship of the Lelos, and they wanted me to jet in with the surveyor while they coasted in silently from another direction. They wanted me to distract the Lelos while they closed in for the kill.

"It worked even better than they had anticipated. The Lelos greeted me like a long-lost friend. Everyone came down to see me arrive in the same ship I'd left in three years previously. I told them I had changed my mind. Diastre came up and said hello. I was startled to see Inman, whom I had left for dead. He held back. He was suspicious, I knew.

"They didn't realize the Andere were near till a party of them blew in a hatch and boarded, sweeping through the ship like a party of marauding wasps through a hive of bees. In one instant a lifetime of calm voyaging came to an end. The Lelos' defense was laughable. Whole acres of the ship were reduced to ashes as the Andere swept up the last pockets of resistance. In an hour there was silence. The Andere systematically rooted through the smoking ruins, flushing the last few pitiful survivors.

"I ran through the ship looking for Diastre. Was I remorseful? No. But I wanted to see her before she was killed. I told the Andere what she looked like. Their chief told me in slow cold tones that if I wanted the woman, I could have her, after she had been sterilized.

"We found her eventually. She had already killed herself, but she hadn't had the heart to kill a baby girl she had clutched in her arms. The Andere allowed me to salvage this one life. They gave her to me, that baby, sterilized.

"Then came the news that there had been an escape. In the confusion, my smaller surveyor had been stolen. The Andere were in an uproar. Part of their command party had been ambushed, massacred. A sunstone was missing. I knew who it was right away. Only Inman could have pulled it off. The Andere left before the smoke had even settled. They were shaken up. They told me they would catch Inman and swat him like a fly.

"They left me there, drifting in a wreck in the middle of the Great Gap. It was a good joke for them—me and an eighteen-month-old girl baby, Alsar, living in the ashes. Inman's child. It couldn't have been mine. But where was Diastre's first baby? In the ashes?" Darlan paused.

"Whose child are you, Chen?" he asked.

"I'm not your son, if that's what you are thinking!"

The Herald laughed shortly. "The idea does not seem to please you very much."

"I doubt if there was ever any love in you. You're a killer. You don't love, you rape."

"That's where you're wrong!" Darlan snapped. "No, I can see you don't understand. Don't make me angry, I'm warning you. Just watch and learn, both of you half-breed aliens." He dropped his eyes and walked out.

Chen went over to Alsar. She was cold, but there was anger in her voice. "He never admitted before that he was not my father. I am glad of it, for I grew up in his shadow, and I know him to the bottom of his heart." She let out a long ragged sigh. "Chen, tell me, what was Inman like?"

Chen looked after Darlan's retreating light. A guard stood unobtrusively outside the door.

Was he? Was he half-alien himself? Was he half-alien and the other half demonic, the son of a genocidal murderer? He didn't look Alsar in the eyes for a long while, and when he did, it was comforting. She was his only touchstone in a hostile and forever homeless universe.

Chapter Twelve

It was 5:05 A.M., and the sun had just risen, cracking open the distant horizon of sea and sky with a thin trickle of red that swelled quickly to flood proportions. The night dew and morning mist burned off quickly. Darlan himself piloted the ship to a landing in a large rolling golf course on the edge of Piedsplat. Only the mechanical street sweepers with their one revolving eye and a few men out sailing to fish in the bay before the traffic of the day noticed Darlan's arrival. The mountainous mass of the ship pressed far down into the sandy soil, and the bulging waist loomed over the buildings adjacent to the golf course as well as an inlet of the bay.

The day was clear, and the weather forecast was for a hot, humid day with thunderstorms in the afternoon. Soon people opened their windows and started to fix a quick breakfast before work. A column of military heliotrucks wound noisily across the sky downtown. People hung out of their windows to get a look, and that was when they noticed the enormous globe of the Ship-That-Gives-Life rising over the highest buildings on the south edge of the city. Soon the switchboards were overloaded. By nine o'clock, not a person in the city was ignorant of the appearance of the mysterious spaceship. Some citizens stopped by to look on their way to work; no doubt they would learn about it in the evening newscast. Many others gathered who did not work, or had taken the day off on impulse.

The ship had already been surrounded by a contingent of sharply dressed and well-armed soldiers. A barbed-wire fence was going up at a distance of fifty yards from the wall of the ship. Within the perimeter the soldiers clustered around their mobile kitchens, eating a quick standup breakfast and gawking at the ship that loomed over them, going up to feel the mirror surface, as smooth and neutral as glass.

The press arrived in a group, piling out of their flitters to ask questions of everyone, poke their microphones through the fence, take movies from every possible angle. Still there was no sign of life from the alien ship. As one reporter remarked sardonically, it might have been the opening scene of *The War of the Worlds.* No one laughed.

The lunchtime crowd came and went. On the TV the round sphere dominated the screen. It reflected sea, sand, sun, and the low line of dark clouds of the western horizon.

At two-thirty a procession of limousine flitters arrived from the city. The ambassadors of all the first-wave planets came, as well as the Ambassador of Earth, who arrived like a dignitary in his own right with an entourage of four flitters and an honor guard of ten armed Dominion regulars in dress uniform.

The diplomats had assembled in a large asphalt parking lot adjacent to the golf course. They had been told no more than the soldiers who guarded the ship— only that a ceremony of welcome was to be held and their presence was requested. Their curiosity would have impelled their attendance at any rate. In the ranks of the diplomatic corps, as in the crowd of idlers, businessmen, schoolboys, retired gentlemen, and mothers with their children, the speculation ran rampant.

Rumors chased each other through the crowd. The ship was obviously alien, though apparently friendly, for the soldiers were protecting the ship from the crowd, and not visa versa.

The diplomats had been instructed to be there at two-thirty, and they were punctual. Darlan let them cool their heels for an hour. At three-thirty a small dark square appeared in the skin of the ship just above the level of the sand. A flitter emerged and settled down to the ground at the other end of the parking lot. It was a government flitter with a large Rimhawk emblazoned on the bottom.

The flitter bounced gently on its grasshopper legs. The door in the nose opened, and from the dark interior emerged a figure the crowd knew well. There was a wave of excitement mixed with anticlimax and disappointment. They had been expecting the apparition of a ten-foot demon from the Late Show. It was Darlan.

However, the public appearance of their Herald was cause enough for excitement, for his appearances were rare. The last time had been over a month ago, when he denounced the murder of his special envoy to Earth by an agent of the Dominions. War had seemed imminent, and then, somehow, nothing had happened. The issue quietly slipped into that file of past memories, a near-crisis that didn't quite make it, and the completion of a new recreational dam soon diverted the public's attention.

Now, as Darlan stood before them again, a serious mood fell over the crowd. Was this to be war? Would next week, tomorrow even, see the planet girded in jet trails as an army of occupation came to ransack their homes and offices? Or was this to be the inauguration of the New Empire in which every citizen of Arcturus (that survived) would become a nobleman in his own right?

The Herald looked with satisfaction over the massive crowd. How they must be curious about this ship and his sudden appearance after a month and more incommunicado. His eyes made a quick survey of the limousines. All the ambassadors were there. They would be sweating it out! Darlan waited till the anticipation of the crowd had charged the air; then he pushed the stud which activated the microphone at his throat.

"My people!" His voice boomed across the packed heads and shoulders of twenty thousand people. The crowd roared back a greeting, a speechless voice like a buzz of static which transfigured the incoherent mob into a united whole, all ears.

"One month ago," Darlan went on, "the Dominions committed an infamous act of aggression against the sovereign planet of Arcturus. I am referring to the cold-blooded, cowardly murder of our special envoy to Earth, Lord En'varid. A member of one of our founding families, he was shot in the back on his return trip to Arcturus. He never saw home. Lord En'varid was trying to negotiate a peaceful settlement with Earth over those territorial ambiguities which have so disrupted our commerce and stunted our economic growth. Lord En'varid went in search of peace, and what did he find?"

"War!" a leathery voice yelled from the back of the crowd. "War!" The people took up the refrain. "WAR!" Darlan let the chant grow for a minute; then he threw up his arms. The crowd quieted instantly.

"For years we have chafed under the autocratic and inhumane rule of Earth. At a time when we were ready to break loose in the skies, to spread our growth to all the nearest stars, she has held us back. She has taxed our commerce, divided us from our sister planets by preventing us from uniting in our common economic interests. Our men must serve in the Dominion armies; our leaders must pay their homage to the Ambassador of Earth."

Darlan let a pregnant silence fall over the crowd as he readied them for the clincher.

"We must harbor no grudges for past offenses. A new day is dawning across the galaxy. A new day! Soon all that has passed will be of little importance. Without looking back, we must break our fetters and take our own path into the future!" He paused to let the cheering subside. The foreign ambassadors were uncomfortable in the midst of the hostile crowd.

"The time has come to change our alliances.

"For the past month I have been gone, far away in space. I cannot disclose where. I was holding a conference with the representative of an alien civilization, and I have returned with good news!"

This time there was no cheering. They had all half-expected it—aliens. But here was the fact staring them in the face. Everyone in the crowd, including the ambassadors, thought, "This is it?" The most momentous discovery in the history of man, and here they were. When the cheering started, it was sudden, shocking, immense. Darlan could not make himself heard for five minutes.

"I need not remind you that this puts you, as Arcturians, in the forefront of the ranks of humanity. Out of all the civilized planets, it is we who have found—and made peace with—the first intelligent alien culture.

"Tomorrow. Tomorrow, a representative of this alien race will make a public appearance at noon in the Civic Auditorium. It will be televised for those of you who cannot attend in person. Tomorrow, the alien and I will each make a statement on the future of our planet, indeed, the future of mankind. I hereby proclaim today a day of national celebration. Go to your homes and take stock of yourselves, for tomorrow is the dawn of a new era!"

Darlan withdrew into the dark polarized bubble of the flitter, and the giant metal insect leaped aloft and flew over the city toward the Herald's official residence. Already, before the crowd was out of sight, he was on the phone, making a succession of calls which would start the Arcturian Army and Navy rolling out their machines of war, already tuned, oiled, and ready for the struggle to control the five hundred planets of the Empire of Man. Darlan would not sleep that night.

Under the cover of the planet-wide celebration which

was filling the streets with spontaneous parades and demonstrations, Darlan's secret police were visiting the homes of certain powerful men and women known to be outspoken against the war, or allied to the Dominions through political or economic ties.

As Darlan's limousine made a last turn over the Herald's spacious residence, Darlan thought how, when he had moved into that antique mansion, he had been filled with pride at his accomplishment. But beside the scope of this undertaking, taking the Herald's office paled to insignificance. Never again would he rule a piece of rock teeming with people like termites. Now he would own the stars even, five hundred and how many more? Not a population, but the whole grasp of mankind. He was more than a man. He was more. Now he realized what awful pleasure the Andere took in killing, and what cold, purposeful emptiness they felt waiting for the moment to come, for the end of the chase to approach.

He remembered Chen and Alsar, and for a moment toyed with the thought of having them killed. But he didn't want to admit he was afraid of these half-breed aliens, one of whom might even be his own son. He regretted admitting his own treachery to them, not because he was ashamed of it, but because he knew they would hold it against him, and it would make it difficult to use them. But they were potentially too valuable to throw away. Alsar had learned all the strengths and weaknesses of the Ship-That-Gives-Life. Growing up on it, she could speak its language better than Darlan himself. The war could not be won without it, he realized. And he could never teach another to fly it properly. No, he might be able to get her to fly it for him still, if he made her a gift of Chen's life.

The flitter came down lightly on the patio. Darlan emerged unassisted and crossed to the glass French doors of the old colonial-style salon. The head of the domestic staff was there in a freshly pressed white shirt and dark red suit.

"Welcome home, sir," he said with a diffident smile.
"Thank you."

The Arcturian Ambassador to Earth arrived home
with no fanfare, not incognito, but unannounced and
unnoticed in the turmoil of that day. His arrival was
duly noted by a subofficial of the customs police, but
his superior did not get around to reading the report
until some days later. The police, the civil air patrol,
the army, and the militia were all being mobilized.

The Ambassador drove to a hotel in the old quarter.
He had one suitcase. His clothes, dated though stylish,
attracted no interest. After a hurried meal eaten in the
privacy of his room he changed some money and went
out to a public phone. He made twenty calls. Only
three were answered. The Ambassador talked briefly
and hurriedly.

The last call was placed to an old friend of the Ambassador's. He spoke frankly, with the Ambassador's
good at heart. "Take refuge in an embassy," he said.
"Or they'll throw you in jail with the rest of us."

The Ambassador shook his head. Soon the embassies
would be no refuge. But he had come expecting this,
come on the chance that there was one last accomplishment he could perform in the service of Arcturus, and
that was to save her from destruction. It had happened
to the Earth. But would anyone survive the cataclysm
this time?

Outside, the short night had just fallen. The Ambassador of Earth was sitting in conference with Bosaven
and the embassy staff when one of his aides interrupted. The Arcturian police were at the gate of the embassy, requesting an interview with the Ambassador.

"What do they want to talk about? Did they say?"

"How many?" Bosaven asked.

"Just three, sir. One came to the door. There are two
others in the flitter."

The Ambassador turned to Bosaven. "Do you think
this is a trap?"

Bosaven shook his head. "I don't think they'd go about it this way if they intended to kill you."

"All right," the Ambassador consented. "Show them in."

Bosaven wished he had his men with him. He felt cooped up and exposed in this building. But he was no safer on the streets. That afternoon, the police had come calling at his boat. He was not there, but John and Ja'in had been picked up, and he didn't dare return to the schooner. Many of his contacts had been rounded up as well. His future looked pretty bleak.

The aide came back in five minutes, leading a tall, tired man in the crumpled uniform of the Dominion Navy. His eyes were bleary. He pulled himself erect and addressed the Ambassador.

"I am Garcia Dal, commander of the *Extrix*."

"What's this all about, Commander? Where are the Arcturian police?"

"They dropped me off and left, Ambassador. For the past three days I have been a captive in Darlan's ship. There was a battle. We had twenty-three light cruisers. We approached his ship in the Great Rift. We demanded they identify themselves, and they opened fire on us. We lost all our ships. I am the only survivor."

"Oh, my God," the Ambassador said.

Bosaven let out a low whistle.

"That's not all," the commander blurted out.

"Afterward, Darlan blew up a sun. He blew up a sun!"

By dusk the crowd surrounding the alien spaceship had swelled to gigantic proportions, as practically the whole population of Piedsplat, and many other towns, came down to see. Many had brought their dinners and picnicked on the beach under the curling shadow of the ship. Most people had brought their portable TV's as well, though for the entire day there had been nothing on the screen except pictures of the ship and the crowd around it. Flitters were coming in from halfway around the planet. Where the bay flanked the ship, a whole fleet of small and large boats, anchored side-by-side, packed like sardines right up to the beach. Cries were constantly exchanged from boat to boat. There was a festive atmosphere, especially among the boat owners, who were sipping beer, relaxing, joking, looking at the florid sun go down.

On the other side of the horizon, opposite the setting sun, a bright new star had just arisen, so brilliant it could be seen in the day. It was the new nova that had made the headlines the day before, for it was in this quadrant. Luckily, it had not been an inhabited system, but a small Dominion Ranger station had been completely obliterated. Already most people had forgotten about it, and seemed surprised to see it there.

As the dark came on, bonfires sprang up around the ship. More than half of the spectators drifted home, late for dinner or early for bed. The rest turned their backs to the cold mist that was creeping up from the bay and enjoyed the warm, blazing fires. Inside the perimeter, the guard was changing.

Around eight-thirty, several people noticed a small skimmer leave the ship, its silhouette sharp against the dark blue sky. It sped silently over their heads and buried itself in the black jagged skyline of the city.

Ten minutes later, while the crowd was still discussing the unescorted and secretive departure of the skimmer, a score of larger aircars swept out of the hatch like a group of angry wasps. The deep-throated roar of the unmuffled engines could be heard long after the military fliers had disappeared into the complex ring of skyscrapers and tree-covered islands which surrounded the lagoon. The hatch remained open for a time, projecting a bright square shaft of light onto the trampled golf course.

"This time, I'm driving the getaway car," Chen had insisted, and now he regretted it as he wove in and out of the maze of small islands and jetties that broke up the lagoon, dodging palms and masts and antennas in a confusing welter of spears and shadows. After several anxious turns of the harbor, he recognized Bosaven's ship and dropped to the water beside it. The small, flat skimmer bobbed lightly, its deck inundated by the small waves. From the air, it would be invisible.

Alsar and Chen climbed a rope ladder with wooden slats to the deck of the schooner, making no noise. They were none too soon, for already a dozen flitters were making erratic passes over the harbor. Chen looked down to the skimmer, where it floated half-submerged in the shadow of the ship. They would have to scuttle it before daylight.

There were no lights on the deck of the schooner, and it was silent except for the slow creaking of the joints. The door to the forward cabin was shut and the blinds closed, but a crack of light showed under the door.

"You wait here," Chen whispered. He crept across the deck, staying in the shadows. On one side of the main cabin a porthole was cracked to let the cool night air in. Chen could see past the edge of the blinds. The anteroom was as he remembered it. On the rattan couch a policeman sat reading a new issue of *Waterboy's*, his legs stretched out across the coffee table. Chen held his breath and put his finger over his lips to warn Alsar. He joined her in the fore of the ship.

"It's the police," he whispered. "I could see only one, but they may have more below. I want you to go down to the skimmer, wait a few minutes, and then hail the ship, loud enough to draw them all out."

Chen took out his small dart gun and sank back into the darkness behind a boom. The night was clear, and the light of the new nova shot across the sky like the light of a full moon.

"Hey! Hello, up there. Hey! Could you give me a hand?" Alsar cried from the wet deck of the skimmer. Her voice carried far across the flat expanse of water. There was a rustle and then footsteps inside the cabin. Hard city shoes clattered on the decking. The door lock rattled, and a short, fat policeman stepped out with a pistol in one hand and a flashlight in the other.

"Hello! Is there anyone aboard?"

"I'm coming," the policeman mumbled to himself. With a perfunctory glance around the deck, he strode to the side of the ship. "Who's that?"

"Oh, hello. My skimmer seems to have conked out on me. Do you have a phone? I'm terribly sorry to bother you. I'm afraid my little skimmer is pretty waterlogged. Do you think you could hoist it out?"

With a sigh of exasperation, the policeman holstered his gun. "Yeah. I got a phone here. Come on up. You alone?"

"Yes, I'm afraid so." She hesitated. "Are you alone too?"

"Yeah. Come on. It's all right. I won't hurt you. I'm a policeman, doing guard duty on this fancy boat while the owner's in jail. Here, wait on. I'll throw you down a line to tie to your skimmer." He turned to find Chen standing three feet behind him with the dark gun leveled at his stomach.

The policeman dropped his glance back to the boat. "Hey, what is this?"

"Raise your hands. Turn around," Chen instructed.

Chen took his pistol and searched the man for any other weapons. He took a ring of keys and a knife.

Alsar came aboard quickly. They led the guard back inside and locked him in a closet.

"Well?" Alsar asked as she rooted in the cupboard of the narrow galley. "I agreed we should find some friends to help us, but Bosaven's arrested. Who else is there?"

"No one that I know of. How about you?"

Alsar shook her head.

"All right, we'll act on our own. But first we need some information." Chen looked through the rooms till he found a TV. He brought it back to the anteroom and propped it up against the wall, falling onto the rattan couch. The first thing he saw was his own picture, and then Alsar's, the two escaped Dominion assassins. It wasn't long before they saw a rerun of Darlan's announcement.

Chen looked perplexed for a long time after seeing Darlan's address to the crowd. He turned off the TV and thought about it.

"That's it. I've made up my mind. There's only one thing to do. We must act on our own. We can stop this war. Without Darlan, it would break apart like an ice-floe in a tropical sea."

"What are you getting at?"

"We must kill Darlan."

"That's suicide, Chen. He's protected, believe me. You got close to him in the ship, but that was blind luck. He's got precautions you couldn't imagine. Besides, you're not a killer."

"Can you think of something better?"

"Yes." She grabbed him by the hand. "Yes, I can. Let's get the hell out of here. Steal a ship. Fly far away. We don't owe them anything. Let them destroy themselves. All of them. Don't you see, Chen? *You're not even human*. I have lived with that fact longer than you—Darlan never let me forget it. I know what it means."

"No. I can't do that, Alsar. I'm not staying out of a sense of honor or conscience. I am fatalistic. We can't let Darlan do it, because there would not be a safe corner for us in the whole galaxy. The Lelos ran away. Did it do them any good?"

"You feel guilty about the Lelos, don't you?" Alsar asked. "You want revenge. All right. We will try, for I want to see Darlan dead. Did I ever tell you how my mother—your mother—died?"

"Tell me later. I don't want to think about that now. Where is Darlan vulnerable? Wait, though. How about the appearance tomorrow? Won't he be surrounded by people then? What do you suppose he meant about this alien? What alien? You don't suppose there actually is an Andere around, do you?"

Alsar shook her head strongly. "No. I'm sure there is not. For one thing, Darlan is afraid of them. Afraid that one day they will change their minds about him and come back to take the ship and kill him, or worse.

He would never let an Andere get near him. No, I think it must be a hoax. The bait that Darlan was using to lure in the big cartels was the promise of exclusive trade rights with the aliens that built this ship. Ironic, isn't it? I can't imagine what he has in mind, but you can be sure it's designed to throw in one more gage against the Earth."

"Perhaps we could shoot him from the audience. With this." Chen brandished the dart gun.

"You'd have to be right next to him. They'll use a magnetic shield in front of the podium. It won't stop projectiles, but it will deflect them."

"A bomb, then."

"Do you want to kill everyone? Besides, how would you place it? Where would you get one?"

Chen paced the floor, trying to work off the pressure that was building up inside him. "What do you think?" he finally asked.

Alsar picked up the knife Chen had taken from the policeman. It had a thin, flexible blade six inches long which recessed into the slim flat plastic handle and sprang out at the touch of a stud. Chen swished it back and forth. In the hand of an amateur, it could cut up the man who used it as bad as his victim. But Chen knew how to use it, for Inman had taught him as a boy. Had it been in Inman's mind at the time, Chen wondered, this revenge?

Alsar went back into the galley to heat up some soup, leaving Chen to thresh and winnow his memories for the grain of truth. An old world, the world of men, had closed its gates to him. And it was Darlan who had thrown him out. Alien. But how could you be alien to yourself? At the same time, a new world had opened up its horizons. The familiar stars took on a new portent. They were alive! His place was out there, as it had always been. But Darlan stood by the gates to that new life, like a watchdog that doesn't sleep. And Chen had to get by. . . .

Outside, the rain began to patter on the decking.

Chapter Thirteen

◆

The next day dawned with elemental brilliance. Darlan watched through the tall windows of his office as the sun rose over the retreating wall of storm clouds. To the east of the Herald's mansion, a stretch of freshly washed dichondira caught the light of the sun, dropping away to the thick shade of a small park.

It had been a short night and one without rest. He had to act fast. His sudden arrival had thrown everyone off balance, and he was seeking to keep things rolling to maintain his advantage. Earth must have concluded that he had backed down now, after the harsh threats of a month past. Now that he was suspected of bluffing, he would act and profit from their indecision.

Darlan took his breakfast alone in his office. He had just received the news of the escape of Chen and Alsar, which his officers kept from him until they had exhausted the possibility of a quick recapture. Darlan tried to focus on what to do with these two troublesome half-aliens, but his memories kept sliding back to Diastre and Inman and the Lelos, those happy, frightened people condemned to a life of flight. He came around the massive desk and threw open the windows. Away in the distant trees, the birds were singing. It calmed him and revived him.

He was still at the window when the first flitter grounded on the dichondira. Four more came down in rapid succession. In each flitter was one man with a briefcase.

For the cartel negotiants the night had been without sleep as well. Most of them had come without break-

144

fast, their minds unresilient after twenty hours of agonizing indecision. Darlan had forced a decision on them
which none of them were accustomed to accept: an
unconditional yes or no that would either ruin them
and their cartels or make them the richest men in the
galaxy.

Darlan closed the window and withdrew into the
room to wait. It was fifteen minutes before the five men
were ushered into his office. They walked straight to
their seats without being invited. An air of cool effi-
ciency masked their anxiety.

The short craggy negotiant from the Antares Cartel
spoke up first. "Since we are all, for the present, negoti-
ating with you as equal parties, Herald, we have agreed
among ourselves that one should speak for us all. To
make things easier, I shall tell you our unanimous decision. We have decided to give you our support, with
certain stipulations."

"What sort of support?" Darlan interrupted impatiently. "Do you mean active or passive support? Are
you going to supply me, or are you going to fight
alongside of me?"

"We will supply you with men, ships, and munitions
to the best of our abilities, while retaining under our
command enough ships and men to assure our own
safety. We will also aid you by debilitating the Dominions through an economic embargo."

Darlan leaned across his desk. "I will tell you right
now, I don't like the idea of bearing the brunt of the
fighting while you wolves sharpen your teeth at my
back. There is only one way we are going to win this
war, and that is if you give me your unconditional support—everything you've got! If you withhold military
support from me, the first enemy I attack will be you. I
will take your cartels apart piece by piece." He paused
significantly. "Sun by sun."

Darlan turned to look out the window. "Now, what
are these stipulations?"

"We wish to be awarded exclusive trade rights with
all stage-two planets in our respective areas, leaving

control of the stage-one planets to you. We wish exclusive trading rights with the aliens. And lastly, we want to negotiate directly with the aliens, not through an intermediary."

"Directly? No. You may have your little monopolies, but if you wish to trade with the aliens, you'll have to deal through me. You have no alternative. This is one control I hold over you. Do you think I'll hand it over on a silver platter? No, it's out of the question."

The negotiants exchanged looks, conferring with the invisible signs they understood among themselves.

"Very well," the Antares negotiant agreed gravely. "For the time being we will allow it to continue as such. However, we expect that in the future the aliens will wish to deal directly with us, thereby getting our goods wholesale."

Darlan smiled dryly. "I doubt the aliens will wish to buy any product you have to offer. Well. Gentlemen, I am glad we have come to an agreement. As you realize, the signing of a contract between us would be a meaningless formality. There is no power in the universe capable of holding any of us to our pact except our own self-interest. I predict you will not be dissatisfied with the results of our alliance. Even without the aid of the aliens, we could sweep the Dominions!"

Darlan pressed a stud on his desk. A servant entered immediately through the side door with a tray of chilled glasses. Another followed with a bottle of champagne in a bucket of ice. The five negotiants broke their awkward silence. They talked about the weather: the streets were littered with palm fronds blown down by last night's angry storm. As their nervous tension dissipated, they looked askance at Darlan as he stood again by the window.

To Darlan, this little victory was the last in a long succession of private triumphs. The next one would not be so private. His name would echo from Aloyus to Thermantle, the length and breadth of the Dominions. Let these merchants have their little concessions now.

Later there would be occasion to weaken first one, and then the next, until they too came under his wing.

The public appearance of the alien was scheduled for noon, but by six A.M. and even before, there were long serpentine queues winding back from the entrance to the Piedsplat Civic Auditorium. In the large square which fronted the building, loose knots of people exchanged gossip on the checkered flagstones. Inside the hall the video crew was already at work. Every cameraman was filled with a sense of his own importance. This would be the most momentous film ever made.

Every person lounging outside in the oblique rays of the early sun was caught up in the significance of the event. Every man and woman felt a sense of participation in history and fulfillment that was not illusory. There were many great powers due to gather in the auditorium that day, and the power of the audience would not be the least of these, but the greatest. Darlan could not launch a war without the consent of his people, but he had gone to them for their approval last, for he was sure of the plebiscite.

A military band was setting up early on the balcony of the auditorium, and the dull, flat voice of the equipment manager boomed, "Testing, testing," across the square.

The crowd was saturated with plainclothesmen. The entrances to the building had been patrolled since the day before by a detachment of the army as well as the city police. Now the guard had been withdrawn from the Ship-That-Gives-Life to take up stations around the auditorium, leaving only a neat perimeter and an honor guard of five men left by the big bay landing door which lay open at ground level. All morning, a steady stream of repairmen and their lumbering waldos had been pouring into the ship from the nearby naval docks.

Seen from the plaza, the Piedsplat Civic Auditorium was a high, imposing wall crowned by a pointed dome.

A single set of massive double doors gave access to the building under a narrow balcony, where the band was crimped against the balustrade. Inside, the auditorium was spacious and opulent. The broad lines of cushioned chairs were broken by rows of shrubs and broad aisles which swept down to the skirts of a huge stage hewn out of a thousand-ton boulder of crystal-clear quartz. Workmen were at work here early in the morning, doing a last touch of cleaning, setting out complementary programs, polishing the ashtrays, and wiping the face of the crystal stage. When the preliminaries were over, Darlan's security force gave the whole auditorium a thorough going-over.

The stage, lit softly from within the crystal, was deserted and unadorned. Here, no paraphernalia was needed. No microphone, podium, chair, or any other accouterment would detract the *presence* of the alien.

The Herald came late to give things a last scrutiny before the audience was admitted. He was not apprehensive. He had perfectly gauged the minds of all his antagonists. He knew their weaknesses, and he would shortly have them in hand. There was only one loose end that still annoyed the Herald. So far there was no sign of the two escapees. They had gone to ground, possibly straight to the Ambassador from Earth. But no matter. What did they know? Darlan had disclosed nothing to them. Alsar knew only bits and pieces, and Chen knew nothing. So Chen had taken Alsar from him, just like that damned Inman had stolen Diastre. When they turned up, they would feel the full weight of his revenge.

As noon approached, Bosaven had joined the small crowd of onlookers that remained by the side of the great alien ship. He sized up the small guard and the large ship. So this was the vessel that had defeated twenty-three cruisers of the Dominion Navy in a single engagement! This was what they would have to fight. It irked him. He knew the Dominion Navy would fight with all the pertinacity and bravery that such a struggle to the death demanded. And he knew that greater men than Darlan would fall before that ball of quicksilver, victims of a machine, a force, that Darlan had not fashioned, but stolen. As long as Darlan was on the loose, no man could wake up and look at the rising sun without a spark of apprehension.

With four men, Bosaven thought, he could take that ship as she sat now, with five guards at the open portal. Or could he? How many more guards were inside? If he could get a bomb inside—one small, very radioactive one would do—perhaps he could hamper Darlan enough at this critical time to swing the balance in favor of the Dominions.

Bosaven turned away from the ship. They were not at war yet, but he felt sure they would be before the day was over. And as soon as Darlan made the announcement, he would be ready, with four men and five bombs. He knew he could get the bombs. The men would be more difficult, for it was a suicide mission. He would have to explain what was at stake. . . .

He shouldered his way quickly out of the crowd. He would have to work fast, and he was glad of it, for it would take his mind off the prospect of his own death.

The aging Arcturian Ambassador to Earth had no invitation to the prime seats of the auditorium. When he arrived, all the seats had long since been filled, but his name was all the ticket he needed. A colonel was ushered out to answer a nonexistent call, and the Ambassador was graciously escorted to his seat. If Darlan had known of the Ambassador's arrival, he would have had more cause to be nervous, but everyone assumed the Herald must already know, so no one hastened to inform him.

The surprise appearance of Lord Intrus, the Ambassador to Earth, quickly drew a small crowd. It had been ten years since he had last been seen on Arcturus. Two generations ago, he had ruled the planet in the days when it was just beginning to form the base of its current prosperity. He was one of the few Heralds who had left the office voluntarily, and this alone had made him a legend in his own lifetime.

The rumor began to circulate that war was surely imminent if Darlan had recalled the Ambassador to Earth. This was seen as a grim portent as the Ambassador's name circulated quickly around the auditorium. From the front row to the very distant back, people craned their necks to get a glimpse of this old man as he sat surrounded by admirers and old acquaintances.

Though he had been gone for ten years, the Ambassador remained a force to be reckoned with in the political arena of Arcturus. Many younger Arcturians looked to him as an example, and many older ones remembered his peaceful, prosperous term of office with nostalgia. The time he had spent away from home had done nothing to diminish his reputation. On the contrary, it had enhanced it greatly, and some of the almost involuntary awe of the Home of Man had rubbed off onto the Ambassador himself. His influence could be both insidious and far-reaching. He had a wealth of contacts among the powerful alliances of the planet, and as a Herald, the first thing he had learned was the art of survival.

The Ambassador was sorry his appearance had caused such a stir, for he had wanted to witness the appearance of the alien from the background. If Darlan learned of his arrival, the Herald would lay traps for him in advance. Though the Ambassador could not stop the planet from going to war, he could divide the public and cause reluctance among some to support Darlan wholeheartedly.

The subdued babble of the crowd was interrupted by the strains of the "Spangled Skyways," the anthem of Arcturus, and the lights dimmed suggestively and then brightened to allow the crowd to settle into their seats. The last of the Ambassador's visitors scurried away.

The lights were cut altogether. A spotlight stabbed at the empty stage, lighting the heart of the translucent rock. For a while, nothing happened. The more seasoned spectators were used to this ploy of Darlan's, and they waited patiently while their neighbors squirmed in their seats, leaning anxiously forward to peer over the shoulder of the person in front of them.

When the time was ripe, Darlan stepped onto the stage. He was dressed in a simple white uniform. He raised his hand to quiet them.

"My friends," he said.

"Today, man finds he is no longer alone. It is not me, Columbus, but rather this not-a-man that you are about to see. He found us.

"The consequences of this new door into the future are yet to be discovered; however, there is one thing that is sure: that door is open to us! To Arcturus alone. We have made the first contact, and we will profit by it. Do we need the taxes and the arrogance of Earth, when, by our own power of industry, of thought, we can create a better life for ourselves and our children? Do we need Earth for a master when we can have all the power of an alien culture for our ally? Yes, our ally. I have talked extensively with the alien, and I tell you I find him to be far less foreign than the unseen, omnipotent autocrats of Earth!

"I came here to remind you of our own ambitions and the future which can lie in store for us, if we take the occasion to act decisively. But I also came here to introduce you to an alien intelligence. I will tell you nothing to lessen the shock of the encounter. Our alien friend can speak our language, and I will let him tell you about himself. I trust you will accord him all the friendly consideration you have given me."

Darlan simply turned and exited. The spotlight was cut. A brief murmur quickly died down, and a feverish silence seized the room. Again, they waited. The audience grew uneasy. People turned to their neighbors with a half-formed question on their lips.

The spotlight came on. A tall, thin silhouette emerged from the light. Very much like the shape of a man, it had two legs, somewhat bowed, with a joint at the knee, and two arms with a hand of six opposable fingers and nothing that could be called a thumb. A monstrous head rose above the narrow shoulders. The skull was more rounded than a man's, hairless, and dull. The hide of the scalp and face was rosy, in some places pale, in others—around the eyes especially—a deep crimson.

But what drew the attention of the audience first and last was the alien's nose, or rather proboscis. It was about three inches thick at the base, and hung down over the mouth, covering it completely. The crimson tip was only a half-inch across, punctured by a wrinkled, obscene hole. It twitched, like a snake, from side to side.

The alien blinked in the light. He straightened the pleats of his short tunic. The first words he said were, "Please, could you dim the lights? They hurt my eyes."

The sibilant voice boomed out over the auditorium. The accent was thick, but hearing this creature produce any kind of recognizable tongue was as amazing to most of the audience as hearing a dog ask to go out. Spontaneous applause broke out. Only his immediate neighbors heard the Ambassador to Earth mutter to himself, "He can't get away with this. No one will believe it."

But the audience was far from doubting the authenticity of the being which stood before them. It was everything they had imagined an alien would be: though bizarre, the alien was more peculiar than menacing—almost cute, some would have said.

"I am glad to have the occasion to speak to so many humans," the alien went on in a slow, meticulous voice, articulating one word at a time, patiently and well, but with the impersonal rhythm of a computer. "To see so many of you together makes me feel there is a future for our galaxy.

"I come from a large world with few people, people as me. For more than a century we have roamed the galaxy, hoping to find some population of intelligent creatures to pass on our age-old knowledge to. For we are dying. There are but a few of us left, and we can no longer bear children. Within another century, my people will cease to exist."

The alien paused to let this sink in. There was a limp silence from the audience.

"But it is not for you to mourn the fate of my people, for our culture will live on, intermingled with your own. Our secrets will become your secrets, our methods yours. You are a very young culture. We are a very old culture, and we wish you to profit from the mistakes we have made. We wish you to profit from the riches of technology we have amassed and which now lie unused and without a future. . . ."

When the alien paused again, the audience could no longer restrain their feelings. There was a mixture of jubilation, amazement, pity, compassion, and elation in the thousand voices which rose against each other, and one after another they sprang to their feet to applaud, cry out their sympathy, and voice their approval. The mass of people abandoned their seats and surged up to the skirt of the stage. The video cameras zoomed in on the impassive, dignified face of the alien. He showed no fear of the people, and rightly so, for it was in no one's mind to hurt him, except . . .

Lord Intrus, the Ambassador to Earth, was the only one still seated in the half-hysterical audience. He was calmly waiting for what he knew would be the concluding half of the speech. Now that the alien had "willed" the remnants of his dying strain to humanity, all that remained was for him to appoint Darlan as the executor of that will. There was little the Ambassador could do now. Darlan's scheme was excellent. In a few months, nothing more would be heard of the alien. He would conveniently disappear, leaving Darlan in the possession of a legendary wealth of technology—and propaganda. Half the Dominions would cede to him, anxious to share in the wealth and afraid to resist. The other half would soon buckle under the brunt of Darlan's massed military. If only he had been here for the last ten years, the Ambassador thought. His contacts, his power, had been slowly but steadily eroded during that time, till now he knew he stood one chance in a million of weathering the coming storm, and scarcely a hope of stopping it in its tracks.

The Ambassador rose to leave. The auditorium was in pandemonium. The alien had raised his hand for silence when the crowd's attention was drawn to a tall, lithe man in the uniform of an Arcturian police officer who had vaulted onto the stage. He approached the alien. Silence fell. The alien turned hesitantly toward the stage exit, and then back toward the man.

As the man stepped closer, recognition seemed to strike the alien. He turned and ran.

Chen brought him down with a flying tackle.

As they skidded together across the polished quartz, a cry of shock and disbelief sent members of the audience spilling onto the stage. Darlan's police came running from the wings with pistols in their hands but could not shoot because of the crowd.

The alien doubled Chen up with a lucky kick, but Chen did not release his remorseless grip on the alien's leg. He clutched him higher, by the tunic, pulling him down. The alien kicked, elbowed, clawed, and pounded frantically as they rolled over and over. A dozen hands tried in vain to pry them apart as the police fought through the crowd. One cameraman, more anxious to see than to help, stood swaying in the vortex of the action, catching the last detail of the struggle as literally the whole population of Arcturus sat dumbfounded in front of their TV's.

Chen held on in spite of the numbing blows that were raining on him from every direction. He never got a chance to pull the knife. He struggled forward till he had a firm grip on the slippery rubber snout of the alien. Suddenly, he let himself be torn off the alien's body.

As they pulled him up off the writhing, prostrate form, Chen felt the nose stretch in his hands and then give way with a loud snap and a cry of pain. As the weight of the crowd bore him back, he held aloft a dangling mass of gray rubber and plastic, with a metal apparatus dangling by its wires. The cameraman zoomed in on the head of the alien, and as the creature turned toward the light and the camera, instead of a gruesome wound, a face familiar to them all filled the video screen. In spite of the underpinnings of the mask, no one could fail to recognize the features of Darlan, their Herald.

With all the actors in the play frozen in the act of discovery, an old familiar voice cut through the embarrassed silence. It was a voice some had known from forty years ago, and now it seemed to bring them back from a waking dream they had mistaken for reality.

"Citizens!" cried Lord Intrus, the Ambassador to Earth. "This outrageous trick is the last of many Darlan has played on you. Can you doubt any longer that he is a sham, a dictator content to use you, to play with your planet, your wealth, and your state in a shameless game of power politics? Is this the man you would go to war for, send your sons, neighbors off to fight for? Is this the man you would break away from the sacred traditions of Earth to follow, this cheap trickster? He ridicules you. Citizens, wake up! There are no aliens. Go to the ship, and you will find only Darlan's men, Darlan's machines, Darlan's masks!"

The audience cried out in rage. They screamed for Darlan's life, and if he had not escaped with his guards even as the Ambassador was speaking, they would have torn him apart on the spot.

From the back of the auditorium, a long cry rang out. "TO THE SHIP!" It was taken up by the crowd. "To the ship, to the ship." The auditorium emptied as quickly as it had filled.

From the Civic Auditorium to where the huge ship was grounded was only a mile or so. The angry crowd poured out of the auditorium like a hive of disturbed hornets, and in flitters and on foot, poured toward the golf course where the great quicksilver ball loomed high and sun-bright.

To the diehard crowd which had never left the side
of the space ship, the events in the auditorium had
passed with all the flair and alacrity of any good video
drama. They were hard-pressed to believe it was real
until the vanguard of the angry mob buzzed down,
their flitters raising a cloud of dust in front of the entrance to the ship. Far away, the murmurs of a swelling
throng reached the ears of these few relaxing picknick-
ers. A small tense crowd gathered at the gate. The entrance to the ship yawned in front of them.

The small detachment of soldiers left to protect the
entrance had not watched Darlan's appearance on the
TV, and they could think of no reason why this crowd
should be gathering here. They little feared any vio-
lence from the same people who had come only the
night before to marvel at the monstrous space ship.
However, they could tell that the crowd was excited,
and they exchanged uneasy glances while their com-
manding officer tried to raise someone on the intercom.
There were no smiles on the faces that pressed against
the wire fence before their post.

Bosaven hung in back of the crowd, perched on the
rail of an abandoned flitter. He knew the mood of the
crowd. He was no less amazed than the rest of them at
the catastrophe of the auditorium, but he knew that if
Darlan escaped with this ship, no planet, no sun would
be safe from his revenge, and Bosaven knew full well
how devastating his wrath could be.

The head of the crowd that descended from the auditorium now heaved into sight around a corner of the
street. They were chanting something that could not be
clearly distinguished in the garble of voices. They advanced like a torrent, spilling over the sandy hills and
the dark asphalt parking lot.

The captain of the detachment was gesticulating excitedly into the intercom, pausing to nod his head and
run his eyes over the crowd. He put down the phone
and called to his men, waving them to retreat into the
shelter of the ship. Bosaven swore nervously to himself.

With the doors closed, ten thousand pairs of hands could not beat them open.

The soldiers backed cautiously toward the door.

"Cowards!" someone screamed.

The first rock flew, catching one guard on the shoulder. All that saved the men from a barrage was a scarcity of rocks in the sandy soil. More objects—shoes, bottles, oranges, portable TV's—flew as the crowd pressed forward, carrying the first rank over the fence against their own will. Two flat cracks snapped the turbulence of shouts. A single scream.

Bosaven gunned the flitter up into the air, spilling off the other people who had been standing on it. The line of guards had drawn up at the door, and they were firing wildly into the crowd, which was milling around as the front ranks tried to escape while those in the rear pressed forward to see what was happening. He jerked the joystick forward and angled the round base of the flitter down toward the doorway. Two bullets tore into the metal base.

Bosaven crashed down jarringly, crushing a guard under the weight of the flitter, knocking another off his feet. The great doors of the alien ship crashed shut on the body of the flitter, digging into the metal like putty. The flitter was crushed, but not severed. The door was open a yard above the crumpled wreck. Bosaven picked up the rifle of the guard that had fallen. Behind him, the crowd stood irresolutely on the remains of the barbed-wire fence.

Bosaven waved the rifle in the air. "The ship is ours!" he cried, and plunged into the dark opening in the gleaming shell.

Five thousand people followed.

A week later, the Ship-That-Gives-Life shone as bright as ever in the late-afternoon sun. A thin wisp of smoke still trickled from a corner of the bay door. The mob had accomplished what twenty-three battle cruisers of the Dominion Navy had failed to do. They had completed the awful destruction begun by the Andere. Large pieces of the ship had been carted off. Fires and secondary explosions from Darlan's stores had finished the demolition—and driven off the last of the scavengers.

Now the soldiers of the provisional government finished reerecting the barriers that the mob had torn down a week before. Now there was another crowd, of mostly the same people.

In a week, the ship had passed from space ship to derelict, from an alien wonder to a national monument. Garish three-D postcards of it could be had at any newsstand. The papers vied with each other in their eyewitness accounts of the fatal and momentous storming of the ship.

This day was a day of celebration as well. A new Herald was being inaugurated, the young and inexperienced protégé of a wealthy family, a distant relative of Lord En'varid. The impressive ceremony was attended by a mob of well-wishers, but there were some notable absences.

Lord Intrus, the Ambassador to Earth, was not there. Nor was Bosaven. Darlan's absence surprised no one. He had disappeared into thin air the day of his downfall.

The *Astrion* made its regular scheduled departure for Earth that afternoon. The Ambassador to Earth was aboard. He would dine every night at the captain's table with five cartel negotiants whose role in Darlan's nearly successful venture he had little cause to suspect. Jerson, cook and sometimes jailer, suspected that these stodgy merchants knew more than anyone about Darlan's disappearance—which the press had been quick to label murder. Jerson had his own ideas, and he kept them to himself.

Bosaven was on that same flight, but he would dine in less impressive company. He was going to Earth on an "all-expense-paid-holiday," as he called it. Chen and Alsar had come to Kelos to wish him off. They owed him more than Chen's freedom, which Bosaven had been quick to see to in the aftermath of Darlan's fall.

Bosaven had also seen to it that they got a good, comfortable, spaceworthy ship. The old man had been frank: "I and everybody else will feel a lot more comfortable if you disappear for a while, preferably a long while."

Chen and Alsar watched as the *Astrion* vanished into the penumbra of Arcturus; then they too turned their backs on that planet for the last time.

Epilogue

It wasn't till decades later that another prospector came crashing through the gas cloud that blanketed Balder-wa. The man was quick to congratulate himself on his find, until he discovered that someone had already set up a beacon on this godforsaken piece of rock, thus preserving it from any other claim for a century.

On this beautiful, disconsolate planet they had left their footprints. They never came back.

☐ **HADON OF ANCIENT OPAR** by Philip José Farmer. An epic action-adventure in Atlantean Africa—in the great Burroughs tradition. Fully illustrated.

(#UY1107—$1.25)

☐ **A QUEST FOR SIMBILIS** by Michael Shea. Through the weird world of the Dying Earth they sought for justice.

(#UQ1092—95¢)

☐ **HUNTERS OF GOR** by John Norman. The eighth novel of the fabulous saga of Tarl Cabot on Earth's orbital twin.

(#UW1102—$1.50)

☐ **THE BURROWERS BENEATH** by Brian Lumley. A Lovecraftian novel of the men who dared disturb the Earth's subterranean masters.   (#UQ1096—95¢)

☐ **MINDSHIP** by Gerald Conway. The different way of space flight required a mental cork for a cosmic bottle.

(#UQ1095—95¢)

☐ **MIDSUMMER CENTURY** by James Blish. Thrust into the twilight of mankind, he shared a body with an enemy.

(#UQ1094—95¢)

☐ **HOW ARE THE MIGHTY FALLEN** by Thomas Burnett Swann. A fantasy novel of the prehumans and the rise of an exalted legend.   (#UQ1100—95¢)

DAW BOOKS are represented by the publishers of Signet and Mentor Books, THE NEW AMERICAN LIBRARY, INC.
